DIGBY'S DIARY

Adventure in the Quarry

Story by Elaine Bird
Pictures by M. Briel

Digby's Diary

Text Copyright © Elaine Bird 2002
Pictures Copyright @ M. Briel 2002

ISBN: 1 903607 47 7

Previously published in electronic format by Instant Books, USA.

Typesetting and Publication by

Able Publishing
13 Station Road
Knebworth
Hertfordshire SG3 6AP

Tel: (01438) 812320 / 814316
Fax: (01438) 815232

Email: fp@ablepublishing.co.uk
Website: www.ablepublishing.co.uk

This book is dedicated to my two sons,
Richard and Timothy, who have
proven themselves to be masters
of their own destinies.
I adore them, and my heart bursts
with pride at their achievements.

Digby

Chapter One

I live in Bulawayo, Zimbabwe, a small land-locked country in southern Africa. I have never had the opportunity to travel abroad and therefore have no personal experience of either England or France. However, I understand that the weather patterns and landscapes of those two countries are vastly different from our own. I believe that during the long winter months in those far away lands, snow falls to the ground in great quantities and rain occurs all year round creating wonderful green scenery. Here, in Zimbabwe, we receive no snow and our winter months are short, dry and mild by comparison. The summers are very hot and long with only a few months of rainy weather. During the long dry months of the year, the bush areas are mostly brown, but when the rain arrives, the countryside bursts into life with wonderful colours, and it is indeed a sight to behold.

You already know my name so I shall begin by telling you about myself. I am a quadruped of French descent with curly, black fur. However, as time waits for no dog, there are sprinklings of silver to be found in my well-groomed *coiffure. I am fortunate to have a very kind English speaking duoped mistress to whom I shall refer from this point on, as "mother". I remember my quadruped mother well and miss her terribly even to this day. My foster has proved to be most satisfactory and has taught me well in my command of the English language, to such an extent, that I have totally lost my French accent!

My quadruped mother was very aristocratic, though I have no recollection of my birth father. I come from a litter of five, myself being the first-born. I remember playing with my sibling puppies in our basket, tumbling around, and growling constantly in an effort to make us sound fearsome. My furry mother was always so loving and gentle, creating a perfect home for our happy family. She spent numerous hours cleaning and suckling us with such affection that the memory of it brings tears to my eyes and a lump to my throat.

Then one day when I was old enough to understand the true meaning of life, that being that family is all-important, I was taken away from my cuddly siblings and adoring mother. I recall how she nuzzled all of us very close to her and I misinterpreted the moisture in her large black eyes. When she tried to explain to us, in a broken speech, that we were going away, I thought it would be for only a short period. We were all so happy where we were, with each other as companions, why then, should we be separated from our beloved mother? The distress I suffered was monstrous and I cried for many weeks asking continuously to be returned to my birthplace, but I never saw any of my natural family again.

The new family who took me in was large indeed, for there were many other quadrupeds of varied descriptions. None of them liked me very much either, which caused further anguish, and they bullied me awfully. However, as I grew and they realised that I would one day be larger than most of them, they began to accept me, until at last, at the present time, I am now in my rightful place at the head of the family, diminished in numbers though it may be.

Mother has always been quite dogmatic about my appearance and insists upon having my fur primped regularly. I actually quite enjoy being preened although I would much prefer not to have them douse me in that cold water first. Personally, I think that Mother enjoys it so, she herself fashions her own fur in much the same style!

I notice that duopeds do not have fur all over their bodies as I do, but only on their heads. That does not seem to apply to the males of that breed, for I have observed that my duoped master and his young pups carry considerable more fur elsewhere upon their physical structures than do the females. It is very sad to note that the pups appear to have left home in much the same manner as I was forced to do when I was just a pup myself. I really do miss them. The eldest is so tall I have come to think of him as my gentle giant. And the younger one is a constant tease. He seems to derive great enjoyment if I place my forepaws on his shoulders and growl ferociously at him. Needless to say, I would cause him no harm, for I have grown to love my entire duoped family dearly.

I am not certain if my natural mother was responsible for having my tail chopped off, but I do not recall any pain. It was such a long time ago and now it is covered with a perfect pom-pom of fur, which looks decidedly appealing. I am definitely able to wag it way faster than any other dogs with longer tails, almost creating a blur of fur, much to the delight of all duopeds.

Whenever one or more duopeds arrive to visit mother, I always give them a warm welcome. My duoped master, whom I shall call "father" because he is so kind to me, appears to take offence to this and I know not why, but I continue in the hope that he will one day understand. After all, barking is the only way I can be vocal and licking is the dog form of kissing!

We all live happily together in a rather large home built on an elevated rocky outcrop, and the numerous stairs provide wonderful exercise. Mother and Father made the home even larger by adding a room that is used far more than any other. The furnishings in this room consist of a long counter with tall chairs around it and there are occasions when many duopeds visit and behave in the strangest of fashions. They all appear to suffer the same affliction of unquenchable thirst, and proceed to pour copious quantities of liquid down their throats. For reasons unbeknown to any quadruped I have spoken to, this causes them to behave most unusually indeed. Some are quite unable to put one paw in front of the other, so it is just as well that they have only two upon which to walk!

This particular room is very special to me too as it houses something that holds my attention for many hours at a stretch. I never noticed it when it was first installed. It is built of the same material as is used in some of the doors, which one can see through, but cannot walk through. One day as I was entering the room with Mother and Father, there was a great splash from inside this transparent box, which attracted my attention. When I glanced up I noticed a strange creature moving gracefully across the width of the structure. I was absolutely spellbound, and have been ever since. I am determined to get that creature out of there one day although I am not too sure what I will do with it when I succeed, but I shall continue trying. Hence, I am prevented from visiting the box without being accompanied by duopeds, but manage to sneak in periodically. I have to confess that I find it extremely relaxing watching the creature, but he appears to take delight in the fact that I cannot get at him. There are times when I become so frustrated that I leap up at the box and try to bite my way through the transparent material, but I always fail.

When the duopeds are in the room I am permitted to watch the water creature for as long as they are present, and I find myself sitting in front of that box for such long periods that I develop an acutely sore neck and back. Of course, this does not deter me, for I find it far more entertaining than watching the duopeds behaving badly.

My greatest responsibility in life is to protect Mother. She spends most of her time during the light hours of the day in a small room at the bottom of the house. Here she sits in front of a much smaller box with a face made from similar material as that of the transparent one which houses the water creature. These furless friends of mine have strange pastimes indeed! I believe that Mother is creating some kind of "work" on this box, though how she could is really beyond my comprehension.

Anyway, I digress from my story. As I was saying, my priority in life is to protect mother and so I always lay directly in the doorway of this little room so that no creature, whether it be another of my kind or furless, can enter without encountering me. I can be quite ferocious when I need to, despite my appealing appearance. I am perfectly capable of making many duopeds stand back and shiver in awe of me.

One morning, Mother was "working" at her little box with her back to the door and I was in my usual sentry position when Father came into the room. I had neither heard nor seen him coming, as I regret to report that I had fallen into a slumber whilst on duty, but am always quick to awaken and take to my post at a moment's notice. However, this particular morning, Father had failed to see me too, probably because my fur is the same colour as the floor.

He was carrying in his forepaw, a bowl, not as large as the one I eat my dinner from, and stepped directly upon me! You have to understand that these duopeds have much larger paws than we do, and are very heavy indeed. I had not realised just how heavy Father was until that moment. I awoke with pain streaking through my body like a bolt of lightning, and leapt to my four paws snapping and snarling, for I knew not what had happened to me. Father also had a terrible fright as he shouted so loud with language that turned the air blue, and Mother screamed in alarm.

What a commotion! Father lost his pawing and began to fall like Goliath, still with the bowl grasped in his forepaw. Remarkably, the bowl did not break, but its contents went up into the air and rained down upon Father almost in slow motion. He was eventually lying on the floor still clutching the bowl and showered with white liquid (something I really enjoy to lap, but very seldom am given) and some sort of brown flakes. I ran outside of the room as fast as my four paws could carry me as I was certain I would be blamed for the disaster, though I was only doing my duty. But, as is the norm, it was only father who insisted that it was my fault, and Mother came to my defence in her usual maternal fashion. I must confess though, my heart was thumping against my breastbone so hard that I thought it would burst through my rib cage at any second.

* * * * * * * * * * * * * * * * * * *

I have been experiencing the most awful sensations in my ears recently. There is this terrible itching feeling right inside and no amount of scratching eradicates the problem. I try shaking my head furiously, so that my entire body rocks, in an enormous effort to dislodge whatever it is in there, but to no avail.

Eventually mother took me to visit a furless friend who used a cold metal object to push into my ears. This did not help one bit! He put some liquid inside and this was continued over a very long period of time. I did not mind to begin with as I was always given a small piece of meat as a reward each time I was forced to endure this indignity, so I indulged them. I was taken back to see this mortal on numerous occasions, but he just could not get rid of these bugs from my ears.

Then, one day, Father took me to see him, and left me there. The next thing I knew, I was back at home with Mother. I have no

9

recollection of being returned to my home and when I awoke there was an awful sick feeling in my stomach. I tried to stand up but immediately fell down again. My ears were tied back, and there seemed to be some sort of fabric wrapped all round my head. I tried with every effort to shake it off, but I was so giddy that I kept banging my head against the floor or the wall. That was very painful!

Finally I was able to stand on my own four paws, but I was so unsteady and weak that I stumbled and tripped. I could not see clearly where I was going for the air was like a haze in front of my eyes, and sometimes I walked right into the wall or some item of furniture. But mother fussed over me like a hen, which I enjoyed immensely.

At last the material was removed from my head, but the pain and itching never left me. The eldest pup had come home for a visit (they both do this every few dog years) and it was his turn to take me to visit that mortal. I was awfully proud for he took me in mother's very special vehicle and I was permitted to sit on the front seat! I stretched myself up tall and proud and watched exactly where we were going. Other duopeds, in other vehicles not as special as the one I was riding in, looked at me with curiosity, but I simply ignored them with my nose in the air!

Regrettably, I still suffer with mites in my ears to this day, and I so wish something could be done to rectify the matter.

* * * * * * * * * * * * * * * * * * *

Let me tell you a little about my existing family. I will not dwell on those who have passed on, as I grew very fond of many of them over the years and it distresses me. Besides mother and father and their two pups, to whom I have already introduced you, there are two other canine quadrupeds and a feline, who I think will be my first choice.

This dear creature has become very aged, but remains princely, though I doubt his breeding warrants such behaviour. Toby is a real character and obviously holds a special place in the hearts of the duopeds, for he is exceedingly spoilt. For some reason this does not perturb me in the least, possibly because he has won a place in my heart too. He is completely grey in colour, though this has nothing to do with his great age, for he has been the same colour as long as I have known him. I consider him very fortunate in this respect, as the natural aging process will go unnoticed upon his fur.

I remember well an occasion when the duoped pups were growing up and we lived in another home. The eldest pup was given a feathered friend as a gift. This poor creature was kept in a cage and Toby showed such interest in it, that it was moved into another room of the house and the door kept closed. I think it was at this time that I learnt a tremendous respect for Toby as he revealed such cunning. The feline species can be sly indeed. I still know not how he accomplished it, but he managed to penetrate that room.

Mother, her pups and a duoped friend were sitting at the table in another room when Toby crept soundlessly in and under the same table. As there were other quadrupeds present he began to growl while he crunched his prey, and the combined noises alerted the furless ones. Regrettably, it was too late to save the feathered creature, as it was only the head that Toby was munching on, but the furor that ensued was a spectacle to behold!

The two pups dived under the table simultaneously only to find a few pretty yellow feathers as Toby took off like a cannon being fired. The pups, who were only young at the time, were right behind him at a sprint, and mother was screaming after them, for she clearly feared that they would slay Toby. Naturally, in my curiosity, I followed and witnessed the feline losing at least one of his nine lives.

He had somehow succeeded in getting himself onto the roof of the room where the vehicles are housed. But he had underestimated the speed and agility of the youngest pup, for he too was up on that roof in almost as quick a time. Before you could say, "jack robin" the youngest pup had Toby by the throat and I could see his eyes beginning to bulge. His calling had begun to sound rather like that of a toad and I was convinced that he had earned himself a ticket to the hereafter.

The eldest pup was still on the ground and demanding Toby's demise with such vigour that I thought I had better steer clear, and moved to stand behind a tree from where I could watch the scene in relative safety. It seemed an interminable age before mother arrived, and in the loudest voice was able to instruct her two pups to release the feline. The youngest pup eventually discarded Toby like a piece of garbage and he tumbled off the roof, but remarkably landed on his four paws! A little shaken and uncertain of his whereabouts, he stood for only a few moments, but that was time enough for the eldest pup to lay his forepaws on him. Had mother not been present, Toby would undoubtedly have met his maker.

As I say, this incident increased my respect for the feline, as he never once exhibited any fear. When he was finally released he shot off into a tree where he remained for several hours. Upon his return to the house, later that evening, he behaved as if nothing had happened, and was consequently reunited with the family unit. This was many dog years ago and Toby would now no more eat a feathered creature than chase it. His geriatric state of mind has rendered him a docile, loving feline with a tremendous sense of humour.

His favourite trick is to hide behind a chair or some other suitable piece of furniture and await a passing creature. He cares not whether it be duoped or quadruped, but at just exactly the correct moment, he lashes out so unexpectedly with his claws, that the unsuspecting passer-by is taken quite by surprise and screams and yelps can be heard many times during the course of every day.

Unfortunately, due to his great age, he is becoming weaker of body, and I know not how much longer he will be with us, so I spend some time periodically helping him with his grooming. A very treasured, furry friend he is indeed!

As Toby is geriatric, so, too, is Charlotte. But a sweeter, more charming little old lady you could never wish to meet. She is a great deal smaller than I, with white curly fur. Charlie, too, has her fur preened each week, though there is very little left of it due to her immense age. But winsome she is after each furdo.

I fear that two of her most important senses are waning, those being that of sight and sound. I recollect an event that made me laugh so that it brought tears to my eyes. Mother and Father had been away for a while and must surely be due home soon. I had heard the neighbour's vehicle arriving at their home and began to bark to attract attention. I felt certain that Mother and Father would soon be home too, as I was quite aware that they had all gone away together.

Charlie came to stand beside me in front of the wall, through which we could see nothing, but I could hear duoped voices. She can obviously hear certain noises like, perhaps, the sound of my barking, for she set forth with her own contribution. She puts such gusto into her efforts that her little forepaws leave the ground with each bark! Between us it became quite a cacophony.

Then I heard another vehicle coming up our own driveway and I knew instinctively that it was Mother and Father returning at last. How I loathe the times that they are away and leave us home alone. Well, I darted off through the trees and over the many rocks, through treacherous terrain, to greet them as they arrived, with exuberant barking.

Charlie had not seen me go, nor realised that the sounds were now coming from a different location, but continued with her welcome at the top of the rocky outcrop facing the wall which separates the two homes, some considerable distance from where she should have been. This continued for some time and both mother and father called out to her continuously, but to no avail. She simply could not see or hear them. It was only after my excitement had abated that I grasped the humour of the situation.

On some occasions too, I have mistakenly growled at Charlotte thinking that she was the other one, to whom I shall introduce you shortly, and she appears to completely ignore me. I always considered this an affront, until I understood that she frankly did not hear those sounds at all. Her great age is definitely taking its toll on her and regrettably I fear that her time with us is limited too. I shall sorely miss her, together with her ugly little face and that tooth which has now grown out of her mouth and protrudes along her upper lip. However, to dwell on such sad thoughts is bleak indeed, so I shall move on.

Ruffles I have deliberately left till last. Oh, how I despise that little canine, a mixed-breed to boot! He is slightly larger that Charlie, but also with white fur and an ego way too sizable for such a mutt. He seems to have a winning way with the duopeds, particularly Mother, and this tends to irritate me more than the dog himself. Regrettably, he is still young and has many more dog years left to him, so no doubt he will continue to torture me.

Mother quite obviously loves Ruffles and he revels in her adoration, only making me the more jealous. There, I have finally admitted it, I am jealous of that half-breed. But one day I will succeed in teaching the spoilt brat a lesson or two. I have tried on numerous occasions, but mother and father always foil my efforts. The feelings are obviously mutual, as we simply do not have a civil word for each other at any time.

The latest episode of my attempts to be rid of this mutt once and for all, came quite unexpectedly. Mother was taking a walk in the garden, as she frequently does, and as is the norm, we three canines, and sometimes even the feline, were strolling around with her. I try to tolerate Ruffles for Mother's sake, but there are times when he pushes me over the edge. This particular occasion was one such incident.

Ruffles darted off into a bush full of pretty white flowers, and thorns, apparently after a rat, an infestation of which is prominent in certain parts of the garden. I must say that he is extremely agile and quick on his paws. I was immediately alerted and went to investigate in a more sedate fashion, only to be greeted with a long, low growl from Ruffles. I was incensed! The audacity of this little canine tore away all my dignity and I lunged at him, grasping him harshly around the neck with my not so small jaws. Mother screamed at us but I paid no heed for Ruffles was quick to escape my vice grip and had launched his own attack. Tedious little creature that he should think he could win a fight with the likes of me!

It all happened so quickly, with Mother still screaming in the background, and I sunk my teeth into his foreleg. Mother was beating me with something and I truly wanted to stop, but each time I let go of him, he was at me again. We had moved our position slightly with our tumbling, and were now on the other side of the bush from Mother. She was apparently in quite a state for she dived across the bush landing directly upon it, in a prone position, and must have had thorns piercing painfully into all parts of her body. Her arms were flailing, uselessly trying to catch hold of me, and I still had to contend with the white mongrel trying desperately to sink his teeth into me!

Just when I thought I had him for sure and was about to do him in, Father rushed down the garden at a pace I never thought he was capable of achieving. He snatched Ruffles from my jaws and Mother was finally able to hold onto me, though still in her prone pose atop the thorn bush. The commotion was over and probably lasted no longer than two or three minutes, but it seemed like an eternity. If only I had succeeded in my quest, but Ruffles had many holes that were not there at the onset, and each one of them seeped blood, so I was forced to content myself with that.

Ruffles

Chapter Two

There are two young duoped pups who call around periodically to the house in order to clean the big transparent box, which is home to the water creature. They always arrive on bi-wheeled vehicles, which make very little sound. I have grown extremely fond of these two, who are friendly and talk to me all the time as I watch, absorbed, while they go about their work. They actually remind me so of mother and father's pups, who, as I have said, are now grown and left home. Their names are Richard and Timothy and they are full of energy. I always look forward to their visits as their laughter is infectious and they both have such fun-loving attitudes toward life.

I remember one occasion when these two arrived, each with a round colourful ball attached to a piece of string and tied to the paw holds of their vehicles. The balls must have been light as they floated directly up into the air, pulling the string taut. The pups untied these balls and removed the string, carefully holding the openings of the balls.

Each took a huge gulp of the air inside the balls and when they spoke their voices took on a strange note, which rendered them helpless heaps of laughter. The more they laughed, the funnier they sounded, which made them laugh even harder. As their voices began to return to normal, they took another gulp of the air from inside the balls until they were completely deflated, both the balls and the pups. I barked my enjoyment and bounded around them for the entire duration.

One day when they had completed their chores and the water creature had been safely replaced in the transparent box, they boarded their bi-wheeled vehicles to leave. The large gate, which secures the property, is undeniably magical for it appears to open of its own accord, simply sliding sideways and then after a short interval, it slides back the way it came and is closed once more. I had followed the pups down the long driveway to the gate and watched with curiosity as they sped off down the road.

It was then that the idea came to me. I simply had to know where their home was, so I took off at a sprint after them. Fortunately, due to my long legs I was able to keep up, but it certainly took all my effort, and after an interminable time, I was beginning to feel dog-tired. The journey appeared never-ending and my flanks were heaving, my tongue almost dragging along the pavement, and my lungs were ready to burst.

Finally, the duoped pups stopped, not as I had expected at their home, but in a bushy area with no houses in sight. I suddenly realised that I had been concentrating so hard on keeping up with them, that I had paid no attention to the route we had taken and consequently had no idea where we were.

Richard and Timothy dismounted from their vehicles and placed them in amongst the bushes so that they could not be seen. I myself was hiding in some bushes a little way back from them, struggling to regain my breath and wishing fervently for a bowl of water so that my tongue might return to its rightful place.

The pups, led by Richard, being the eldest and largest of the two, crouched down and crept forward through the bushes until they came to the edge of a clearing. I followed stealthily behind, not wanting to attract any attention to myself, and stopped a few yards to their rear, well hidden by the thick undergrowth, my flanks still heaving. I could hear the pups talking to each other in a whisper, about the place before them. It sounded like they had described it as a 'quarry', a word I had never heard before.

Just then there was a scuffle behind me in the bushes. I got such a fright that I spun around bearing my teeth at the intruder, only to find Ruffles with a sheepish grin on his face. He was in a far worse state than I, for his short legs must have had to work three times as hard as mine. I was amazed that he had been able to keep up and a slight stirring of respect for this mutt obscured my vision for only the briefest moment, and then was replaced with anger.

"What are you doing here?" I growled in a low voice.

"I wanted to know where you were going." He managed to reply between heavy panting.

"You shouldn't be here..." I began, but was interrupted by the sound of rustling.

"Richard," said Timothy, "Digby and Ruffles have followed us here!"

Richard crept towards us and reached out a paw to me, which I licked happily, hoping to convey my apology, not only for my presence, but also that of Ruffles, though I know not why I should apologise on his behalf. I was surprised to note that both of the pups were quite delighted to have us with them and they petted us most affectionately.

"But what're we gonna do with them? They might blow our cover," said Timothy.

"They look pretty exhausted to me," said Richard "so I don't think they'll be chasing rabbits for a while."

"They might even prove to be useful," suggested Timothy.

"Yeah, as long as they don't get in the way," said Richard.

"Maybe they can sneak in there for us," offered Timothy.

"And what're they gonna tell us?" asked Richard scornfully.

"I dunno," replied Timothy, "but they seem quite intelligent, maybe they can protect us then."

"That sounds more like it," said Richard.

They then turned and went back to the edge of the clearing motioning us to follow, Timothy with one appendage of his forepaw across his lips in a gesture I still do not understand.

Now that we were at the edge of the clearing I could see huge sand dunes with no vegetation and I wondered what we were all hiding from, for I could see no sign of life anywhere else but where we remained crouched. I wondered if this was perhaps the 'quarry' about which the pups had talked, but not knowing the meaning of the word, I was somewhat confused. Surrounding the perimeter of the clearing was a distinct tree line that followed on from where we were hiding. Everything appeared normal to me, with birds singing in the trees and the odd scurry of small creatures in the undergrowth. Then from a distant part of the clearing I could hear duoped voices, although I could make out nothing that was being said. "Ssshhhh......," said Richard, making the same gesture with his forepaw that Timothy had made earlier, and which still had me bewildered.

Suddenly I heard the roar of a quadruwheeled vehicle and we all shrunk further back under cover of the bushes. I could hear no more voices and after a short period of time the vehicle sped over one of the dunes directly in front of us with dust plumes billowing out behind it. The vehicle had large wheels with thick, wide treads, obviously designed for working out in the bush rather than in the towns. It left the ground and seemed suspended in the air momentarily, landing with a thud, and bounced rather unsteadily, I thought, before continuing its' forward rush, still churning up dust in its' wake. It occurred to me that, whoever was driving it, must have been in great haste indeed. I could not understand where the vehicle had come from, for it seemed to shoot out from the very ground upon which it was travelling.

As the vehicle darted past us, I spied two duopeds in the front seat and Timothy said, "That means there is still one left behind." I deduced from this statement that the pups had been watching the place for some time.

"What d'you think they're up to?" asked Richard.

"They're obviously up to no good. I think they're hiding something down there, maybe drugs or something," suggested Timothy.

"If they are, we'll have to be jolly careful," said Richard, "they'll probably have guns as well then. We could be in danger."

"Maybe that's what they're hiding down there," said Timothy.

"Well, whatever it is, it's illegal, 'cause they're acting really suspicious," said Richard.

"Let's sneak up and have a look," suggested Timothy, ever the daring one.

"OK", said Richard, being equally adventurous, "but follow behind me and keep down!"

Alarm bells rang in my head, with thoughts of the pups getting themselves into grave danger.

So with Richard ducked down low in the lead, Timothy, with the same posture at his flank, and me close to their heels doing a leopard crawl, we set off into the open. Ruffles had held back for just a moment, and then with tail wagging he bounded out noisily from the undergrowth and shot past us all, kicking up clouds of dust as he went, apparently oblivious to any peril that may await him.

"Ruffles!" called Richard in a low voice, "come back here!"

Ruffles skidded to a halt and spun around, still with his tail wagging in great spirals. Where he found the energy is beyond the margins of my comprehension! He waited for us to catch up with him and after further reprimand from the pups, he sulkily fell in behind me.

As we approached the dune over which the vehicle had sped, Richard and Timothy fell to their bellies and snaked their way to the top of the slope. Being a quadruped, I was unable to emulate their actions exactly, but I tried my best and was pleased to note that Ruffles too was now making an effort.

We were in a position to peer over the top of the dune, and I was amazed to see the greatest hole on the other side of it. It appeared to be very deep with quite steep sides and I wondered how the vehicle had successfully negotiated such terrain. This was obviously why it had shot up over the dune, after having to take a run at it. But on closer inspection, I noticed a track running around the inside edge of the deep crater, a few metres down, and running around to the other side. This track stopped directly in front of what looked to me like a cave, not a large one, barely sizable enough for a duoped to enter.

As we watched in silent awe, an immense duoped emerged from the cave, crouched low so as not to bump his head, his body fairly filling the opening, almost unfolding himself! He stretched his limbs and shook his paws as if to regain use of them after being cramped in a small enclosure for too long. He glanced around and seemed to be staring directly at us so we all ducked our heads in unison.

After a short interlude we peeped up over the dune once more and the duoped was busy with something in his hands. From this distance it was difficult to distinguish what exactly he was doing until he raised the object to his ear and I realised what was happening. I could hear him talking but was unable to discern the words he used.

"He's got a cell-phone," said Timothy, stating the unnecessary, "I wonder who he's calling."

"Well, I don't think he saw us or he wouldn't be looking so calm," announced Richard.

"Maybe he's arranging a pick-up," suggested Timothy.

"We've only ever seen the one car coming here," said Richard, "so I don't think anyone else will come here to fetch anything. We'd better keep our eyes and ears open though, just in case."

"We've got to find a way to see inside that cave," said Timothy.

"I know," replied Richard, "but it's pretty difficult to get there unseen."

We watched the duoped talking for some time, his left forepaw waving expansively. His voice was raised and I still could not make out exactly what he was saying, but managed to pick up only one word, "million". The pups, not having the acute hearing that we canines have, apparently could make out not a word.

"I wish I could hear what he was saying," said Richard quietly.

"I can't wait to find out what they have hidden in there," said Timothy, getting agitated.

"I don't know how we're going to get close enough though, unless we are sure that all of them are away together, but I think one of them is always there to guard whatever it is," replied Richard.

"Look, he's going back inside," said Timothy as the large duoped folded himself up again to re-enter the small opening.

"Maybe if we work our way around the outside," suggested Timothy.

"Maybe, but not today, we'd better get out of here before the others come back," whispered Richard, a suggestion I relished for I sensed dreadful evil.

So without further ado or question from any of us, we snake-crawled, then crept across the way we had come, back into the relative safety of the bushes.

"It's getting late," observed Timothy as he looked at the timepiece just above his forepaw "we'd better be heading home 'cause we still have to take these dogs back"."Yeah," said Richard "let's get going."

The pups found their bi-wheeled vehicles exactly where they had left them and climbed on, taking off immediately at high speed along the makeshift road, their hind paws working frantically at the pedals. Ruffles and I raced along behind, struggling to keep up. The bush finally gave way to a proper road and the pups slowed down to a speed that allowed us to trot at a more comfortable pace.

Now there were a few houses along the roadside, which I had not noticed during my hasty outward-bound journey. Apparently neither had Ruffles for he kept stopping and sniffing at the ground, marking his territory here and there, as if in doubt of our route, and ensuring that should we ever need to, we would be able to find our way again.

Standing at the gate of one of the houses we passed were two beautiful golden quadrupeds of almost the same height as myself, but considerably heavier. Ruffles immediately pranced across as the golden male shouted hello in the friendliest of fashions. I was becoming anxious to get home, but had no wish to appear rude, so I trotted across to them after Ruffles.

The male was indeed a good looking dog with a large square head and intelligent eyes. He was definitely well fed as he carried way more weight than he should, but his coat was smooth and shining. He had a hint of a smile on his face and his eyes glittered with mischief and humour. I liked him immediately.

The female was grossly overweight, but her coat was also sleek, a sure sign of a healthy dog. Her head was much smaller than the male's, but the eyes were huge and dark. Soft, gentle eyes that told of great love and kindness.

"Hello," said the golden male again just as friendly "my name is Fred and this is my sister Wilma. What are your names?"

Ruffles responded with his usual exuberance before I was even able to open my mouth to speak and said, "Hi, I'm Ruffles and this is my friend Digby!"

"Friend indeed!" I thought, but greeted them with an amicable "Hello."

"Hello," said Wilma in a quiet feminine, almost timid voice.

"What have you got in your mouth?" I asked, as the sight of her speaking brought to mind something father had once mentioned of a duoped who spoke with a plum in her mouth, making her sound like a snob, whatever that might be.

"It's a stone," replied Wilma slightly embarrassed, as she lowered her head and allowed the stone to drop to the ground.

"She's a real treasure, is my Wilma," said Fred, "she loves to carry little gifts of stone or leaf around in her mouth. Don't be embarrassed little sister we all have our traits. She has such a soft mouth, she could carry an egg around and not break it," he added, addressing us.

"Fred's the treasure really," declared Wilma. "Whenever duopeds come to visit, he always takes anything they are carrying in their paws, into his mouth and leads them inside the house. If they are not carrying anything, he takes them by the paw and physically pulls them along. Sometimes, the bags or parcels he takes on are so large or heavy, he has to drag them along the ground," she concluded with a smile and we all had a little chuckle.

"What breed are you?" asked Ruffles, being ignorant through no fault of his own, I conceded, but still lacking finesse.

"We're golden Labradors," replied Fred, "and you?"

"I am a standard French poodle" I managed to get in before Ruffles.

"And I'm sort of a mixture" admitted Ruffles, "my mother was a Maltese poodle and my father a fox terrier" he proudly announced.

"That explains his impudence and lack of manners," I thought to myself having never before taken the time to ask of his breeding.

"You're very lucky to be out and about, but I've never seen you along this road before," said Fred.

"No," I said, "this is our first outing, and very interesting it has been."

Ruffles proceeded to tell them of our adventure and the Labradors listened with polite curiosity.

"That sounds cool," said Fred, "perhaps one day I will come along with you and see for myself."

"That would be tremendous. Do you ever manage get out from behind this gate?" I asked.

"Well, I've never tried, but there is a smaller duoped gate over in the corner of the garden which is sometimes left open. Maybe one day I'll venture out with you, though I don't think Wilma will come along," answered Fred

"Yes I would," said Wilma with shy indignation.

"It'd be such fun," put in Ruffles excitedly.

"Hey, you two, come on it's getting late," called Timothy, obviously frustrated at being unable to understand what we were saying to each other. We all said our good-byes and Ruffles scampered off towards the pups. I followed a little more soberly as I would not want the Labradors to create an incorrect impression of me.

We passed many more homes with many more quadrupeds of endless descriptions standing at the gates, all of whom greeted us along the way. I was observing all the landmarks as we went for I felt certain that the pups would be going back to the 'quarry' and I was not about to let them do so alone.

I was beginning to feel decidedly weary when I realised that we were getting close to home. The neighbourhood was becoming familiar and I felt greatly relieved. Ruffles on the other hand seemed to have a limitless supply of energy, "Oh! What it is to be young," I thought.

The sun was sinking low in the reddening sky as we approached the gate and I wondered how the pups were going to get us back to the correct side of it. There is a small metal box perched atop a post outside the gate and it was to this that Richard went directly. He pressed a button and a familiar ringing tone sounded. I was watching the proceedings with great interest and then, remarkably, mother's voice emitted from that box and said "hello?" Richard spoke back to the box from where mother's voice had come and replied politely "Hi, your two poodles are outside the gate.

"Oh, thank you, we have been frantic with worry!" she said.

With that, the gate began to rumble aside and I rushed forward, now impatient to get home and with a rejuvenated vigour. When there was barely room enough for my slim body to squeeze through, I made a dash with Ruffles close at my hind paws. I almost forgot my manners so stopped abruptly to turn around and say cheerio to the pups, just as Ruffles ran directly into my haunches, almost knocking me to the ground. I grumbled at him as I watched the pups, with laughter on their lips, wave their paws at us and ride off down the road and around the corner out of sight.

We both scampered up the long driveway side by side increasing our speed when we spied mother standing at the bottom of the stairs waiting for us. She dropped to her knees and cried, "Where have you two been? And look at the state of you, you're a mess, burrs everywhere!" We were so excited to see her that we leapt at her together and she tumbled to the ground laughing and petting us simultaneously. What a glorious moment that was!

Mother gave us some water, which tasted like nectar and then some food, which we wolfed down hungrily. I was now feeling tired indeed and yearning for a sleep when Toby strolled up in that aristocratic fashion and sat down before us, erect and regal, his long tail curled around his forepaws.

"And where have you two scoundrels been?" he asked in that haughty, but affectionate voice, his luminous eyes watching us carefully.

"We decided to explore the world," I replied "and quite an adventure it was too."

"Together, as friends?" inquired Toby sarcastically.

"We just happened to bump into each other along the way." I retorted rather sharply. "Now, if you wouldn't mind, I am tired and would like to take a well deserved nap." I added. Then feeling a little remorseful, I continued with a more friendly tone "I shall tell you all about it in the morning when I am fully rested." I had no doubt in my mind that young Ruffles, with his endless stamina, would give his account of the day's events to Toby and Charlie long before that, but I was too exhausted to care, so I made my weary way downstairs and fell into my well padded basket. There are still three baskets together, but the other two have been vacant for some time now, so I sleep alone. I think I was in slumber before my eyes were even closed.

Toby

Chapter Three

Bright and early in the morning, feeling refreshed, I ventured out into the crisp cold air to perform my daily ritual. The grass was damp with dew, which only invigorated me the more, despite my stiff limbs. I thought about the preceding day and decided that I had better seek out Toby and Charlie to relate my version of it.

The three little ones are fortunate enough to have their beds inside the house, and a small opening at the base of the door through which they can go in and out in order to perform their daily rituals. Unfortunately, I cannot even get my head through this hole, but father was up and about at this time of day so the door was already open.

When I ventured inside I found the three of them still sleeping soundly upon the furniture, something which has regularly annoyed me, as I am not permitted to do the same.

"Hey, you lazy lumps," I said in a loud voice to wake them.

Ruffles jumped off the furniture immediately, but Charlie obviously required further prodding to be wakened from her slumber, and Toby barely stirred.

"Wake up!" I shouted.

Toby opened his eyes lazily and stretched luxuriously, yawning at the same time, and Charlie jumped with fright, almost rolling off the furniture, but catching herself at the final moment. She was attired in a delightful polar-neck jumper, which mother wraps her in during the cold months of the year, as her fur is so sparse. She looks quite enchanting in it I must say.

"Do you want to hear my tale or not?" I asked.

"Oh, I suppose so Digby, though we have already heard Ruffles' story," answered Toby lethargically.

"Well, gather around friends and I shall begin," I said, ignoring his indifference.

Toby, taking his time, jumped off the furniture and sat facing me, those brilliant eyes locked onto mine. Charlie took a little longer to get onto the floor being somewhat arthritic, but finally sat herself down beside Toby obediently. Ruffles, tail swishing like Bazil Brush as usual, moved rapidly to the other side of the feline and the three of them looked as if they were watching a show. Father was in the room and stared with gaping mouth, obviously disbelieving the scene before him.

I concluded my story, to which Toby had listened intently, and Charlie had struggled to hear with her head cocked to one side. I had spoken as clearly as possible, but I am not certain how much of it the dear old lady was able to pick up. She was polite enough to sit quietly throughout the proceedings though, which is more than I could say for Ruffles who constantly interrupted me, putting his own two cents in every now and then.

"Do you intend going back there?" asked Toby.

"Naturally," I answered, "I would not leave those pups to their own devises, something terrible might happen to them. And having listened to their conversation, I have concluded that they have every intention of returning. I sensed great danger there today and I do not think that those three duopeds are very friendly. I have no idea what it is they are hiding in that cave, but it must be of great value."

"I'm coming too," said Ruffles immediately.

"Definitely not!" I responded, "You would only get in the way as you did yesterday."

"You might need my help," said Ruffles defensively.

"Help from the likes of you, indeed," I scoffed.

"Don't be unkind, Digby," demanded Toby, "he could well be of use to you, and I don't think it's such a good idea you going out there on your own."

"I will not hear of it!" I said contemptuously, and left the room as gracefully as I could under the circumstances, my head held high.

Later that day I was sitting down at the bottom of the garden in front of the gate wishing it to open. Mother and father had each driven through earlier, but always waited for the gate to close before driving off down the road, so I had not been able to slip through unnoticed. I had spied Ruffles hiding amongst the flowers, ever watchful, and thought to myself, "stupid dog, with that white fur he can be seen so easily amongst all those colours". The day was long and passed uneventfully. The magical gate never did open to allow me passage, though I waited there until mother and father returned in the evening.

The following day I was up with the birds again, and as father was preparing to leave, I decided I would follow closely behind his vehicle so that I could not be seen. Sure enough, I was able to sneak through and ducked into a bush just outside the garden, thus preventing father from spotting me. Suddenly Ruffles dived through the tiny opening at the last moment, with only an inch to spare, before the gate closed.

I was so angry I wanted to slay him right there, but Toby's last words to me echoed in my ears, so, as soon as father's vehicle was out of sight I took off at a gallop hoping that Ruffles would not keep up and eventually turn back. Of course, he knew the way just as well as I, so although I left him far behind, I knew he would catch up with me.

I galloped along the road at a rate of knots, not once looking behind me. I had decided to outrun the little mongrel and that is just what I intended to do. I had been going for some time and was beginning to flag, weariness taking its toll. Eventually I slowed down and finally, feeling rather mean, I stopped to wait for him, knowing he would take a while as I could see only a white speck in the distance. As he drew nearer I could make out his long fluffy white ears flapping up and down as he ran, he really looked quite comical and I could not help but chuckle at the sight of him. When he did arrive at my side and looked at me with those doleful eyes, I felt nasty indeed. He was too out of puff to say anything, and I could not bring myself to scold him, so I simply waited for him to regain his breath, my own having already returned to normal.

"Thank you for waiting for me," he said between puffs, when he was at last able to speak and innocently unaware of my unkind plan to slip away from him.

"I thought I told you not to come with me today," I responded in as friendly a voice as I could muster.

"Sorry, Digby, but I had such fun yesterday, I just couldn't resist coming along again today," he said.

"Well, I suppose now that you are here, we had better move along," said I, thrown off guard a little by the apology, and thinking to myself that I was indeed mellowing in my old age.

We had only completed approximately half of our journey, and I could see just up ahead to the left of the road along which we trotted comfortably, another canine standing peacefully behind a gate. She was a large dog, taller even than I, and very broad about the shoulders. She had greeted us along our return journey yesterday as had many others, and today she appeared to be waiting for us so we went across to speak to her.

"Good morning," she said, "you're out bright and early today".

"Hi, there," replied Ruffles with that infuriating lack of breeding.

"Hello," I said with a little more dignity, "I am Digby and this is Ruffles".

"My name is Jamie, and as I can see you are looking at me quizzically, I am a Harlequin Great Dane, which is why I have the grey and white markings on my body, and pinkish eyes".

"You have a beautiful coat indeed," I put in, for it was smooth and glistening, the colours blending attractively together.

I noticed that the gate behind which she stood was not as tall as the one back home, perhaps only half the height.

"Is your gate magical," I asked.

"Magical?" she queried.

"Well, does it open by itself?" I added.

"Oh, no," said Jamie, "this one has to be opened by a duoped."

"Are you ever able to get out onto the road," I questioned further.

"I've never tried, but I should think I could jump over this gate without too much difficulty. I haven't really given it much thought, why do you ask?" Jamie responded.

"I was just curious," I said "we had better move on now, but will stop by again and have a longer chat".

"Cheerio then," she said cheerfully.

"Bye," that was the half-breed again.

I gave my farewell and off we went at a brisk trot.

"Why were you asking all those silly questions?" asked Ruffles when we were out of Jamie's earshot.

31

"They were not silly questions," I retorted "and I have my reasons, which I am not prepared to divulge at present."

We continued our journey in silence, Ruffles a little sulky, until we reached the Labradors, where we stopped for a brief, but pleasant tête-à-tête. Ruffles cheered up instantly, and for the second time that day, I found myself feeling remorse for my treatment of him. Fred and Wilma are indeed friendly dogs, and both have such a tremendous sense of humour that they are enough to brighten even the dullest of days. I have found that after each visit with them, my spirits are lifted.

Finally we managed to drag ourselves away from their companionable conversation and trotted along in a friendlier manner until we reached the bushes where Richard and Timothy had hidden their vehicles so recently. We both put our noses to the ground and sniffed the entire area, searching for fresh scents of spoor, but the pups had obviously not been back.

"That is very good," I said " we have arrived before them".

"Why is that good?" asked Ruffles.

"Because our duty is to protect the duopeds," I answered, rather exasperated, rolling my eyes as I spoke.

"But how can we protect them if they're not here?" he asked.

"If they are not here, Ruffles, then we are spared our duty for the time being," I replied feeling rather irritated.

"Do I have to teach this mutt everything?" I thought.

"Come along," I said a little more kindly, "let us go to the 'quarry' and see what we can see".

We padded off quietly through the undergrowth, disturbing lizards and other small creatures of the bush, until we reached the edge of the clearing where we stopped and very carefully scanned the area for signs of the other duopeds we had seen only two days before. It appeared that the place was deserted and there was no indication of the vehicle having passed by recently.

"All right Ruffles, we will leopard crawl to the top of that dune as we did before, but please be quiet today," I directed.

"OK," he replied sounding quite excited at the prospect, his eyes bright and his ears pricked up in his eagerness.

When we were in position, we carefully peered over the top of the dune, but there was no hint of life. I began to relax and only then realised how tense I had become. I scoured the landscape trying to arrive at some strategy, thinking long and hard. My mind was working over the suggestion that Timothy had made, for I could come up with no other ideas of my own.

"What're you doing?" asked Ruffles breaking my concentration.

"I am thinking, so keep quiet for a moment," I replied.

I allowed my eyes to roam leisurely over the scene before me, but the only movement I detected was the drifting of sand from an occasional light wind flurry.

"Right!" I said having come to a decision, "I want to see what is in that cave. However, if we take that track, which is obviously how the duoped's vehicle reaches it, we could find ourselves trapped. So, I think we should skirt the entire perimeter of that great hole around the outside, as Timothy suggested, until we are above the cave. Then we can search for a way down to it and that will provide an escape route as well should we need one."

"Right!" said Ruffles, his Bazil Brush tail wagging annoyingly.

"Bear in mind though, we are not one hundred percent certain that there are no duopeds around and, of course, should they all be away, they could return at any moment," I added quickly, afraid that he may give us away with his youthful exuberance.

"What if we do bump into one of them?" asked Ruffles.

"We shall simply deal with it when the time comes, if it comes," I replied.

"What if they've got guns as Richard thinks?" asked Ruffles again.

"Oh Ruffles," I said exasperated, "I really do not know all the answers, but I am certain that something will come to mind when the time calls for action."

I backed down the dune until I was sure that we could not be seen from the other side and Ruffles followed suit. We trotted comfortably, finding the going easy, but the distance was more than I had anticipated. When I thought we must have been getting close to the cave I stopped, motioned for Ruffles to stay put, and carefully crawled to the edge of the great hole. I was astonished to find that we had only covered half the distance and made a mental note of that should we be forced to make a hasty retreat. I returned to where Ruffles was sitting, waiting impatiently.

"Still quite a way to go," I said.

I judged what I thought must be an equal stretch travelled and stopped once more. Again I motioned for Ruffles to remain where he was, not wishing to draw any unwanted attention to our presence by the use of speech. Ruffles was becoming noticeably agitated and I was fearful that his excitement would prove to be our downfall. His youth might be an advantage in certain circumstances, but at this moment, I required maturity from him, and alas, this he lacked.

Once more I leopard-crawled to the edge of the great hole and almost shed my fur coat when Ruffles suddenly appeared at my side, obviously unable to contain himself any longer.

"What can you see?" he asked with such juvenile excitement.

"I told you to stay where you were!" I growled in a low voice.

"Can you see the cave?" came his eager voice from my side, totally ignoring my retort.

"No, so I would think that we must be fairly close, perhaps even directly above it. Scout around as quietly as you can and see if you can find a way down to that track, I will be doing the same."

Ruffles moved off in the opposite direction and only moments later appeared once more at my side.

"I've found a wash away just over there, but I'm not sure if it goes all the way down," he announced proudly and in not too quiet a voice.

"Well done," I acknowledged grudgingly, "let us have a look."

I stood for a long moment sizing up the wash away before making my decision.

"Alright," I said, "I will go down first, but do not follow until I give the signal."

I gingerly placed my forepaw at the top of the wash away and began my descent. The sand was loose under paw and it made me wonder how goats manage with hoofs that must slide more easily. I was almost at the bottom where it met the track when I heard the sound of crumbling earth behind me. I turned in fright just in time to see Ruffles skidding down, having lost his paw hold. He was travelling at such speed that he knocked my hind legs out from under me and we tumbled together, landing one atop the other on the track not too far below. I was infuriated. I rose to my four paws and shook the dust off me, about ready to teach him a lesson in the art of obedience.

"Will you never take an instruction correctly?" I grumbled too loudly.

"Sorry," said Ruffles with that sheepish grin on his face again, obviously enjoying himself.

I glanced around warily to establish the location of the cave and found that we had in fact travelled a little too far. The cave was to our right with the great chasm behind us, and the track here was too narrow to allow the passage of a quadruwheeled vehicle. In fact, we were lucky, for had we tumbled just a little further, we would surely have landed at the base of that great pit, and there is no telling how fit we would be after a fall of that magnitude. I looked at Ruffles and could see by his expression that there was no need to demand silence, his eyes were alert, his ears pricked.

We padded quietly toward the cave and as we were drawing near the entrance we both instinctively put our noses to the ground. I scented trouble and glanced sideways at Ruffles who had stopped with one forepaw tucked under his chest and his tail out behind him, level with his spine. I was quite impressed, as I knew this to be the stance of a pointer and could not fathom where he had learnt such a trick. I also knew that he too had smelled the fresh spoor of duopeds, but not any we knew by scent.

We edged forward, side by side, both silent, toward the opening of the cave. We craned our necks around the side of the cave together, Ruffles' head being much lower than mine due to his shorter legs. Ruffles suddenly whimpered in terror and I was thrown back on my haunches, growling fiercely, as a duoped lunged through the opening, grappling to take hold of one of us.

I found my paws quickly and threw myself at the duoped who now had Ruffles in a tight grasp despite his continuous struggles and fearsome snarls. I sunk my teeth into the duoped's forelimb, as he lay stretched out across the ground on his stomach, and he immediately released Ruffles, at the same time emitting a howl of pain. With my teeth still implanted in his flesh, I shook my head from side to side determined to inflict as much suffering as possible, thereby, hopefully, enabling our escape.

Something came down across the side of my head so painfully that for a moment I was stunned. I withdrew my teeth and shook my head in an attempt to regain my vision and other senses, all of which were momentarily alien to me. Ruffles was at my side instantly, his tail between his legs and his entire body quaking violently.

Slowly my vision returned and at first all I saw was the blurred outline of a large duoped looming over and directly in front of us. I shook my head again and could feel warm thick liquid trickling from my ear where the blow had struck. Ruffles had not moved from my side and I sensed that despite his terror he would leap to my rescue without hesitation. Small as he is, it was reassuring indeed.

The duoped, whose right forelimb was bleeding profusely, was large indeed with a protruding belly. He had small evil eyes, which right at this moment smouldered with hatred. As he held his left forepaw over the wound, I noticed something in that paw. My vision was clearing rapidly now and I realised that he was holding a gun, just as Richard had feared! I automatically retreated, being well aware of the lethal results of such a weapon, and Ruffles kept close to my flank.

Suddenly a second duoped erupted from the cave and rushed to his partner's assistance. He was slimmer in stature with an enormous amount of fur about his face, much the same as father wears, but not as tidy. This fur was long, scruffy and somewhat dusty. His eyes were a little kindlier, though not so much that I felt at ease in his company.

"What the devil...?" he shouted.

"I'm gonna kill them!" said the first through clenched teeth, as he raised the gun, pointing it directly at my head.

I still had not regained all of my senses and so the split second which might have allowed our escape, had passed.

"Hold it," said the second duoped, placing his own paw over that of the first and forcing him to lower his weapon, "you fire that thing and half the world'll know exactly where we are."

"Look what they did," said the first, indicating his wound.

"It'll heal," said the second, "besides, they're only poodles, it can't be as bad as all that. And judging by the looks of that black one you've done sufficient damage already."

"They might be only poodles, but they've got teeth!" said the first viciously.

"I don't think they'll attack," responded the second.

It occurred to me that we might be out of danger for the moment and I spoke quietly to Ruffles.

"Stand your ground Ruffles, prick up your ears, wag that glorious tail of yours and put on that soft soppy expression you always muster for mother," I whispered.

In spite of the circumstances, and to my total surprise, he obeyed to the letter, although his little body still quaked. I admired his courage and was in awe of such emotions, which I had never experienced before.

"Look at that," said the second duoped, "they're quite friendly, you obviously just startled them."

"I'd like to throttle them," said the first.

"Leave them be," said the second, "they'll wander off and we'll probably never see them again. Come on back inside and I'll see what we can do with that wound."

With that, they both turned and disappeared within the cave.

"Are you ok?" asked Ruffles with concern in his voice.

"Yes, thank you, I'll be alright once this ache in my head subsides," I replied.

"I think we had better get out of here right away, before something else happens," I added. "But I do not think we will be able to climb back up through that wash away, the earth is too loose. We had better make our way as quickly as possible along this track and hope that the vehicle does not come over the rise before we get out of here."

I stood on my four paws a little unsteadily and cocked my head to one side to try to alleviate the pain, but it only worsened it. I groaned and began to put one paw in front of the other tenderly, as each paw step, no matter how gingerly I took it, shuddered through my head making it throb. Ruffles padded along quietly beside me not saying a word, but glancing at me every now and then to see how I was doing.

We finally reached the other side of the great hole where the track rose sharply up and over the dune. I was exhausted and in great pain, so I stopped for a moment to regain my composure before attempting the steep climb. It was then that we heard the vehicle approaching. If we remained where we were, we would certainly be run over the edge of the great hole, and there would probably be insufficient time to get over the top before the vehicle began its descent. It was simply not worth taking the risk, for we knew not how far away the vehicle was. It would mean inescapable death if we met it half way up the incline.

I looked around frantically, my head pounding, but could see no escape.

"Over here," said Ruffles nudging me gently and heading toward the end of the track where the ridge narrowed, but should provide enough space for the two of us to stand if we were careful. We had only just arrived in our little sanctuary when we saw the nose of the vehicle coming over the dune very slowly. When it reached the track along the ridge it was a tight turn indeed, not a manoeuvre to be taken too hastily or the vehicle would surely plunge into the depths below.

We watched as the vehicle, with only one occupant as far as I could see, continued cautiously along the track and we made our way back to the steep incline.

"I think we will have to take a run at it like the vehicle does," I said, unsure of how stable the ground might be.

Ruffles looked at the slope and then at me. Without saying a word he took off at a gallop, his tail streaking out behind him. Half way up the slope he began to slow and his running became bounding leaps as he struggled to reach the top without stopping completely. When finally he reached the summit, he turned around and looked down at me.

"Come on Digby, you can do it," he called a little out of puff.

I took two deep gasps of breath and tried to ignore the pain in my head, then began my ascent as fast as my four paws could carry me. With my head thumping and my paws not grasping the loose earth properly, I slipped, fell over to my side and slid all the way to the bottom again, knowing that had I tumbled I would unquestionably have rolled over the edge.

This was so out of character for me as despite my age, I have always been fit. This injury must have taken a greater toll on my well being than I had thought. I regained my four paws and looked up at Ruffles.

"Now you know what you're up against, you'll make it," he called encouragingly.

I prepared myself once again but this time took a much longer run-up. The pain was drumming in my ears all the way, but I was determined to make it this time. My limbs ached and my paws sometimes slid, but somehow I made it to the top where Ruffles was dancing around in excitement to welcome me.

"Well done, well done Digby!" he said heartily, jumping about like a puppy.

My limbs quivered from the effort and my mouth was dry. My head throbbed and I thought I would collapse. The sun was directly overhead now as I looked over my shoulder to where the vehicle had stopped just outside the cave.

"We had better get out of sight," I managed to say softly through the pain.

Ruffles pranced around me as I laboured toward the bushes for cover, but I was too tired to have it annoy me. We made slow progress across the compacted dunes and when, after what felt like an eternity, we reached the shade of a few trees, I lay down gingerly upon some fallen leaves to rest my weary bones.

Ruffles sat beside me, a worried look on his face.

"What you did back there was great, Digby. I'm so sorry you got yourself hurt in the process," said Ruffles.

"It was nothing," I replied noncommittally, "but right now I just need to rest for a while," and with that I closed my eyes.

I know not how long I had slept, but when I was wakened by the sound of voices the sun had not moved all that far across the sky.

"It's Digby and Ruffles," said Timothy, "and Digby doesn't look too good."

"What's happened old boy," said Richard in a gentle voice, crouching down to pet me.

I lifted my aching head and licked his paw affectionately. Ruffles sat beside me, his brush of a tail wagging excitedly at the sight of the pups.

I wondered how we were going to make them understand that they were in grave danger and looked at Ruffles for assistance. He sensed my concern and gave one sharp bark to attract attention.

"What is it sport," asked Timothy, reaching out to Ruffles who turned and ran through the bushes toward the hiding place of the pups' vehicles.

"Where's he off to," queried Richard.

In an instant Ruffles was back, gave another bark and took off again in the same direction. He repeated his actions a further three times.

"I think he wants us to follow him," suggested Timothy, "come on Digby, you'll have to come along."

"Hang on Tim, we haven't even had a look at the cave yet. Whatever it is Ruffles wants to show us can wait until we head for home," said Richard.

"OK, lets go and have a look then," responded Timothy eagerly.

I let out a yelp of alarm, worried sick for the pups' safety, knowing full well that they had no idea what peril lay in wait for them.

"It's alright old boy, we'll be back shortly. You stay here," said Timothy, and they both turned and made their way to the edge of the clearing.

"Ruffles, do something!" I demanded from my half sitting, half standing position.

Ruffles darted off through the undergrowth and out into the clearing ahead of the pups, where he sat staring at them and gave one sharp bark. Richard and Timothy stopped in amazement. They called him to them, but he would not budge, which baffled them further, so they edged forward. Ruffles ran from this side to that as if he were herding sheep, and would not allow the pups to pass.

"I don't think he wants us to go there," announced Timothy.

"That's why he was running backwards and forwards all the time, he was trying to make us leave," said Richard with sudden understanding.

"There must be something that frightened them down there, and maybe that's how Digby got hurt," declared Timothy.

"Well, let's take them back home. There's enough daylight left for us to come back after that and see what this is all about," said Richard.

I had by this time risen unsteadily to my four paws and glanced across at Ruffles who was now sitting in his sentry position, ears pricked. "He learns quickly," I thought grudgingly.

"If I put on a big act, and move slowly, there will not be sufficient time for them to return," I offered, "so let us get moving."

In fact, I knew that this would not be an act at all, for I was feeling poorly indeed, but I was not about to let Ruffles know that. The pups retrieved their vehicles, which they pushed, obviously aware that the return journey would be slow, and Ruffles and I followed along behind them.

We were walking at an easy pace when we arrived on the paved road where the houses came into view and the pups began to walk a little faster, still pushing their vehicles. I was very pleased that they had decided not to mount them for my body was feeling quite broken.

Fred and Wilma were standing at their gate, golden tails wagging from side to side. As we drew nearer, they put more effort into their greeting and their rear ends began to wag along with the tails.

"Hello again!" called Fred, "are you two alright?"

Ruffles sped across to confront them with the day's adventures. I took a little longer, treading carefully. By the time I had reached them Ruffles had gabbled out enough of the story to produce lines of worry across the Labradors' foreheads.

"You must be in need of some water," observed Fred when I was close enough to hear.

"Indeed I am," said I.

"The small gate which Fred told you about is open today. Why don't you come inside for a moment and have something to drink," suggested Wilma in her quiet voice.

"That is very kind of you, will you show me the way?" I asked.

As I headed toward the small gate set in the wall a few meters ahead, and almost concealed by an overgrown hedge, I heard the pups talking.

"Now what're they up to?" asked Timothy.

"I think they're deliberately stalling," remarked Richard.

Once I was inside their garden, Fred and Wilma led me directly to a large pond. The water was crystal clear and icy cold. I bent my head to drink and it tasted so good that it reminded me of mother's milk. Fred and Wilma immediately waded into the water up to their ample chests and invited me to join them. I wasted no time accepting their invitation and the freezing water did wonders for my aching body. I stood there for a few minutes allowing the cold to seep into my bones before reluctantly clambering out. The water poured off my fur and I shook long and hard to rid myself of the remaining droplets, which stubbornly clung to my coat. It felt wonderful! Ruffles, who had partaken of the refreshing drink, had declined the dip, and watched fascinated as the three of us enjoyed the water.

When we emerged once more from the small gate, Richard and Timothy were waiting for us, somewhat impatiently.

"Thank you both, I feel so much better," I said to Fred and Wilma, " now I must put my acting talents to the test, and appear to be in agony once more," I said, "Cheerio now!"

"You're welcome," said the Labradors in unison, "Bye-bye you two."

"Bye," called Ruffles already half way down the road with the pups who were still pushing their vehicles.

As happened the previous time, all the dogs along the way greeted us excitedly. It made me think of walking down the aisle of a jail with all the prisoners behind bars. One of the inmates to our left was a delightful golden cocker spaniel, very majestic in his stance. He was an intelligent looking animal and his little stump of a tail wagged faster even than my own was capable of doing. We passed quite close to his garden so I could see the warmth and trust in his large dark eyes as he barked heartily. His ears, set low on his head, were covered with long silky fur. I made a mental note to stop and chat with this friendly fellow upon our return.

The day was not yet spent when we arrived at our own gate, so the sky had not begun to redden, but the sun hung low over the trees and I hoped this meant that it would be too late for the pups to return to the 'quarry'. Richard pressed the button on the box atop the post as before and I heard that familiar tone once again. It was not mother's voice that came out of that box this time, but I recognised it to be that of the maid. After Richard advised the nature of his visit, the gate rumbled sideways and Ruffles and I trotted through together, stopping to bid the pups farewell. Very pleased that we had made it home before mother and father, so they would probably have no idea that we had even been out, I made immediately for my basket. I had no sooner closed my eyes than Ruffles arrived with Toby and Charlie in tow.

"I hear you've had rather a traumatic time," said Toby.

"He saved my life and really hurt that duoped bad," announced Ruffles gleefully.

"Oh, it was no more than any dog would have done under the circumstances, merely instinct," I responded, dismissing his comment with some considerable embarrassment.

"So, have you two finally made friends then?" asked Toby curiously.

"He proved to be of some assistance," I grudgingly admitted, "and I must concede that he displayed courage at the time when it was required. Though, had he listened to my direction, the duopeds might not have heard our approach," I added trying to cover up my unexpected praise of the mutt.

"How is your ear?" enquired Charlie loudly, apparently unable to hear even her own voice.

"Oh, it will mend, thank you for asking," I replied kindly.

"You should probably have mother look at it when she gets home," declared Toby.

"No! I do not want them to know that we have been out again or they will make it impossible for us to leave the next time," I said, "so please do not draw any attention to me.

"It sounds to me as if all this is way too dangerous, Digby, and I don't think you should be going back, even with Ruffles," admonished Toby.

"It is because of the danger that we have to go back, Toby, in order to protect the pups, which as you know is the most important function of any dog," I replied.

"Well, do be careful, both of you, I would be distressed should anything more serious happen to either of you," he muttered quietly, perhaps a little flustered by his show of affection.

"That we will be," I promised, inadvertently including Ruffles in our next expedition.

Mother and Father arrived home shortly after that and I bounded up to greet them in my usual manner so that they would not become suspicious by my non-appearance. Neither of them noticed the now dried blood on the side of my head as it was hidden by the flap of my long ear. I was finally able to curl up in my basket and sleep deeply for the night.

Chapter Four

There is an abundance of bird life in our garden, which is not surprising with all the indigenous trees, a large variety of palm trees and great expanses of luscious green grass, cropped short. It was the sound of all these birds singing in the trees which infiltrated my dreams, making them all the more pleasant as I was gently awakening the following morning.

"Digby!" shouted Ruffles.

"What...?" I started, as I bolted upright in alarm.

"Sorry," said Ruffles, "but I've been trying to wake you for ages and was getting quite worried. I was beginning to think you had gone into a coma or something."

"Where did you learn words like that? I doubt you even know the meaning of 'coma'," I grumbled, feeling a little irritated, having been so rudely aroused from my peaceful slumber.

"Of course I do, or I wouldn't use it," he replied indignantly, "Anyway, it's quite late and father will be leaving for work shortly. I thought you might want to sneak out behind his vehicle as we did yesterday."

I was fully awake now and scratched my right ear with the claws of my hind leg, finding some of the dried blood still attached to my fur.

"I think today is the day that the pooch preeners come around is it not?" I asked, speaking more to myself than to Ruffles, "If we miss that, mother and father will become suspicious indeed, so I think we will follow their vehicle out of the garden once we have had our fur done," I concluded.

"I hate having my fur done," said Ruffles grumpily.

I stood up feeling thoroughly refreshed, all my senses having been fully restored, and trotted across to the green grass, which still had the remains of earlier dew. I completed my morning ritual and decided I had better try to get the dried blood off my fur so as not to draw any attention to myself. I bent my head down sideways to a clean patch of grass and propelled myself along, scraping the side of my head. The dampness assisted, but I continued for some time to be certain that I had removed all of it. Of course, I was unable to view the results of my efforts for myself, but was confident that I had succeeded in my quest.

The pooch preeners arrived later in the day before the sun had reached its full height. No comments were made about the swelling on the side of my head, so I assumed that it had not been noticed. Once their job was done, they packed up their gear and made their way down the driveway. Ruffles and I followed carefully after the vehicle and as it passed through the gate, we slipped out and ducked behind the same bush I had used to conceal myself before, this time with Ruffles close at my flank. The magical gate rumbled shut and as the vehicle rounded the corner further up the road, Ruffles and I emerged from our hiding place, both sensing a thrill at the day's events ahead of us, and feeling perky after our fur do.

We took our usual route and stopped outside the gate of the golden cocker spaniel who was watching our approach with a comical expression upon his friendly face.

"Wow, don't you two look handsome today," he observed as we got within hearing distance. Standing beside the spaniel was a tiny grey poodle I had not noticed on our previous journeys, evidently because of his size. It was like looking into a diminutive mirror for this little pooch was identical to me in every respect, barring the colour.

"Thank you, kind sir. This is Ruffles and I am Digby," I said.

"My name is Snoopy," responded the spaniel.

"And I'm Pepierre, Pepi to my friends," announced the tiny poodle proudly.

"I have never seen a poodle of such small stature," I observed politely.

"I am what the duopeds call a 'toy poodle'," he replied.

"Do you mean that you are fully grown?" I asked, incredulous.

"Oh, yes, I'm not a pup by any stretch of the imagination," answered Pepi happily.

Snoopy

"Are you two ever able to leave your garden?" I queried.

"Without a doubt," said Snoopy "this gate is a knock over. Watch."

With that he stood on his hind legs, placing his forepaws against one leaf of the gate. He pushed his snout under the latch and flicked it up into the air. At the same time Pepi nudged the other leaf of the gate, which moved easily toward Ruffles and I on the other side of it.

"There!" said Snoopy triumphantly.

I was very impressed and said as much while the four of us got to know one another using the ritual method of all dogs, sniffing.

In the next-door garden I spied yet another Maltese poodle, larger than Charlie, but smaller than Ruffles. An uglier dog I have never before seen. His eyes were small and dark, but the most prominent feature by far was his teeth. His lower jaw extended further than did his snout, and protruding from that jaw was a row of tiny sharp teeth reaching almost up to his nostrils, for his lower lip did not cover those incisors. His fur was white but a little matted and he looked unkempt. He was standing on the other side of a fence and watching us with interest.

Whilst the four of us were getting to know each other, this little mutt must have been working ferociously, burrowing his way beneath the fence, for he suddenly appeared in our midst with not too friendly an attitude. His presence became apparent to me when I heard the scratching of earth and turned to find him scraping his hind legs in the manner of a bull about to charge. Ruffles stood directly in front of him, his tail up in the air, ears pricked, a stance I recognised immediately as his fighting pose.

"Hold it right there you two!" I growled sternly, "I do not know who you are little fellow, but take my advice and do not mess with Ruffles. Trust me, he has terrier in him."

"That doesn't scare me," said the intruder.

"Then put your paws up," said Ruffles dangerously, flexing his muscles, "and let's see what you're made of."

I moved between these two combatants in an effort to quell an inevitable war and they began to circle me, both growling and snarling at each other.

"Will you two stop it?" I shouted fiercely.

"Not until I've proved myself," said Ruffles menacingly.

"We already know what you are capable of, Ruffles, so back down right now!" I said. He glanced sideways at me and then over at the intruder.

"What's your name anyway?" he asked.

"What's it to you?" responded the intruder rather rudely.

"We've been making friends all along this road and you're the first we've met who's not friendly, so what's the buzz?" went on Ruffles.

"This isn't your road and you shouldn't be here!" said the intruder.

"I don't believe it's your road either," replied Ruffles, "so just introduce yourself and lets all try to be friends."

"Well done Ruffles," I congratulated him, still standing between the two of them.

"I'm Oscar, who're you?" he conceded a little irritably.

Following the ritual of formal introductions, the five of us now relaxed into a friendly conversation.

"Sorry about that," apologised Oscar eventually, "but where I come from I was taught to be as unfriendly as possible to strangers. I've had some nasty experiences. One day I was nearly torn to pieces by a dog much bigger than me."

"So why did you come out looking for trouble then," asked Ruffles, baffled.

"I guess I've just never gotten over it," he replied.

"Well, we are no longer strangers Oscar, so can I take it that we are all now friends," I asked.

"Sure thing," he replied amicably.

"I can see that I do not need to ask if you can escape your garden," I said.

After a lengthy chat about this and that, Ruffles and I bid farewell to our three new friends and moved along the road.

"Why do you ask every dog we meet if they can get out of their gardens?" asked Ruffles.

"I have my reasons," I replied and left it at that.

Further up and on the other side of the road was Jamie calling to us, so we made our way over to her.

49

"Hello boys!" she greeted, " you two look quite dashing! I want to introduce you to a friend of mine."

Beyond a fence separating the two gardens stood a splendid Rottweiler. She was not as tall as I, but the same colour except for brown markings on her eyebrows. She was so broad about the chest that she would prove to be a frightening adversary should one ever come across her in a challenge, so powerful were her shoulders. Her magnificent head was broad too, with strong looking jaws of mammoth proportions. But her eyes were large and friendly, belying her appearance of ferocious and deadly might. Her stump of a tail wagged as we drew closer.

"This is Buddy," Jamie introduced us.

"Nice to meet you," said Ruffles politely.

"My pleasure, I'm sure," I remarked, an expression I had heard one of the duopeds using and rather fancied for myself.

"How do you do," said Buddy most graciously in a warm, feminine voice.

Her eyes were alert and intelligent, her silky coat shining in the midday sun.

"I have been watching you two these past few days and Jamie tells me that you are embarking on some adventure or other," said Buddy.

Ruffles and I launched into a detailed explanation of our recent escapades, to which both Buddy and Jamie listened intently, occasionally interrupting us with questions regarding the contents of the cave.

"Could I come along with you today?" asked Buddy in due course, "the fence at the back of the garden is dilapidated and I can easily get through, but you would have to wait a few minutes for me to get around to the road at the front."

"I can see no reason why you should not join us," I offered.

While we waited for Buddy, Jamie chatted amiably, telling us of how she had been rejected from her former home as a result of her thieving. She explained that she simply could not help herself and stole food if it had been left out, even if she felt no hunger for it. Her great height aided her considerably with these indiscretions and her

50

previous master had tried every conceivable form of punishment in an attempt to rid Jamie of her bad habit, but regrettably without success. Finally, in desperation he passed her on to her current home where she is extremely happy and seems to have outgrown that terribly addiction.

Buddy arrived and the three of us said cheerio to Jamie, then trotted off down the road together toward the 'quarry'. As we paced each other comfortably, Buddy chattered away about her earlier life.

"When I was just a pup I was removed from my mother's care and taken to a foreign home. The very day that I arrived, feeling gloomy and missing my family immensely, I was run over by a very heavy vehicle. The wheel went directly over my hindquarters and crushed both of my legs. My new mistress was in a terrible state and rushed me off to visit another duoped where I was left for many weeks, 'hospital', I think is the name of the place. My two hind legs were tied up tight in some really hard material so that I could not bend them, nor could I stand on them. When I returned to the home where the terrible accident had happened, my legs were still bound up in this hard material, but I was able to get around. I had to be very careful though, because I found it slippery going. As I was growing so rapidly at that youthful time of my life, it was necessary to have the bindings constantly replaced, but eventually they were removed permanently and for the first time I was able to use my legs properly."

"Over the years I have developed what I have heard my mistress refer to as 'arthritis', a terrible affliction, which causes much pain. However, it appears only to affect me when I have been sleeping or resting so that the pain shoots up my spine whenever I try to get myself up from a lying or sitting position. I have now learnt how to do that without quite so much suffering and once I am up on my four paws, I am quite fine!" she explained.

"What a terrible thing to happen," I said. "We have a little poodle in our family who also suffers from this arthritis, but that is because of her great age." As Buddy was finishing her tale, we were approaching the home of Fred and Wilma, who were waiting for us with tails wagging as usual. I had come to enjoy those two cheerful faces and we cautiously crossed the road to introduce them to Buddy.

"How're you feeling today?" asked Wilma, a look of concern on her face, "you're looking quite elegant if I may say so," she added shyly. I noticed a stone on the ground just in front of her forepaws and had a little chuckle to myself.

"Very well, and thank you," I answered both of her questions.

"We saw those two pups going by not so long ago," announced Fred, "and they looked as though they were in a hurry."

"Oh, no! I had hoped we would arrive ahead of them today. Still, if we hasten, we may be able to prevent them from doing anything foolish. Come on you two," I said, "let us move on!"

We found the pups' vehicles and moved stealthily toward the edge of the clearing, not wanting to startle Richard and Timothy. There was no sign of them, so we all put our noses to the ground to find which direction they had headed, Buddy having picked up their scent from their vehicles as we passed. We were pleased to note that they had taken off to the right along the tree line and not out into the open, so we followed hastily, constantly sniffing to ensure that we were on their trail.

The bush was thick and offered ideal cover, so there was no chance of us being detected. We encountered the usual animal life, with insects chirping here and there and were fortunate enough not to meet up with any snakes, for it was wintertime and they always hibernate. At one stage a rabbit bounded out of the undergrowth, startled by our approach, and Ruffles took off after it, darting among the bushes. But the rabbit was too quick for him, and he eventually returned to us, out of puff, but still excited.

We must have gone half way around the' quarry', still within the tree line and so quite a distance from that great hole itself, when we suddenly lost the scent. The three of us sniffed around in every direction, but the scent simply stopped at the base of a tall tree. Quite unexpectedly, we heard Richard's voice from above and we all looked up to find both of the pups clinging precariously to branches high up at the top of the tree.

"It's only Digby and Ruffles!" said Richard, apparently having not noticed Buddy.

"There was such a noise, it sounded like an army following us!" declared Timothy.

In our haste we had evidently created quite a din scurrying through the dead leaves and undergrowth.

The pups clambered down the tree quite deftly, making it look easy, but I doubted I would be capable of doing the same, as my paws were not equipped with the appendages that they had. They jumped the remaining few feet, landing firmly on their hind paws, and it was only then, I think, that they spotted Buddy, for they threw their backs against the tree trunk with a gasp of alarm, not daring to move a muscle.

Buddy wagged her stump in greeting, but the pups said nothing, still not moving. Buddy edged closer slowly and Richard and Timothy stiffened, obviously terrorised.

"I think you are scaring them Buddy, let me see if I can persuade them that you are friendly," I said, "so be still a moment."

Buddy moved no further, still wagging her stump, apparently quite pleased with the reaction she had received. I edged closer to the pups and finally nudged them with my wet nose, wagging my own pom-pom happily. Ruffles went over to Buddy and rubbed up against her forelegs, and then together they approached me cautiously.

The pups visibly relaxed and crouched down on their haunches with paws outstretched.

"She must be a buddy of theirs," said Richard not realising the funny side to his statement.

Buddy came closer until she was near enough to sniff their paws and they petted her tentatively.

"Well, now we've got another ally," said Timothy cheerfully, "so what next?"

"We'll carry on around the tree line until we reach that cave," announced Richard boldly.

"Then what?" asked Timothy.

"Don't know yet, we'll have to play it by ear," Richard answered.

When Richard was satisfied that we had gone far enough, we made our way to the edge of the clearing. We all peered out from the undergrowth and scanned the area seeing no movement nor hearing a sound. Ruffles and I knew that we were indeed in the right place for we recognised the terrain, and it sent a shiver down my spine. We crept up to the brink of the 'quarry' in the same fashion as before, except that Buddy was unable to crawl like the rest of us due to her arthritis. Nevertheless, she was indeed stealthy, for which I was grateful.

We were now on the opposite side of that huge chasm and could see the track as it rose steeply and disappeared behind the dune, close to where we had originally spied on the duopeds, so we must be almost directly above the cave. As Richard and Timothy crept right up to the ridge, so did we three canines, all in a row. Not a word was said by any dog or pup, silence was instinctive. I could see a wash away in front of Ruffles, but it was not the one we had slid down the previous day. I peered over the edge and could see the track tapering to the right, which meant that the cave must be virtually beneath us. The pups, too, peered over the edge, but in so doing Timothy dislodged a clod of earth which pitched over the side and down onto the track noisily.

"Sorry, Ruffles!" I said as I roughly nudged him forward and down the wash away. He slithered to the base and took a tumble, looking back up at me with an expression of utter astonishment on his face. I could almost see the question mark hanging above his head as one sees in a cartoon. Immediately he landed on the track, I launched myself down the same wash away, landing almost atop him, but he scrambled away in the nick of time. Glancing quickly over my shoulder, I was able to ascertain that Buddy and the pups had withdrawn and could not be seen from where we were.

"What'd you do that for?" grumbled Ruffles crossly.

"Had to, no time to explain now," I responded tersely as I saw, with relief, the duoped with all that facial fur, emerge from the cave.

"Now what're you two doing back here?" he asked, not unkindly.

Ruffles did his Bazil Brush act and put on that soppy expression without even an instruction from me! Together we moved carefully closer, hoping to get a look into the cave, but it was too dark to see beyond the opening from where we stood.

"Go on, get along with you, scram!" said the furry faced duoped. We stopped where we were and Ruffles tried some more of his charm by rolling over onto his back, exposing his belly, an action only ever exhibited in a situation of total trust. I could almost see his little heart beating in his chest and knew that there was no trust here, only the necessity of appearing as if there were. Once again, his courage had impressed me and I was unhappy with that realisation.

As 'furry face' bent down to scratch Ruffles' tummy I took the opportunity to slip behind him and peep into the cave. In the gloom I glimpsed the form of a duoped lying upon the ground, motionless, and my hackles rose along the full length of my spine for I sensed something sinister in the air. I sniffed the cold dank atmosphere and was alarmed by a familiar scent, though at that moment I could not place it to any particular duoped. Before I was able to get any closer, Fur-Face stepped in front of me, blocking my view.

"Ok, get outa here now, scat!" he demanded, waving his paws in the air as he spoke.

Ruffles leapt to his paws and we both took off along the track at a brisk trot. Again I glanced over my shoulder to see if I could spy the pups and Buddy hiding behind the dune above Fur-Face, but there was no sign of them and I felt relieved.

We made our way around the great pit and I dreaded the climb out along that steep incline, but was surprised to find that it was not as difficult for me as it had been the day before. Once we were out of the 'quarry', we padded across the dunes and into the undergrowth surrounding the clearing. The pups' bi-wheeled vehicles were still hidden and we could scent no spoor of unknown duopeds.

"Well done, Ruffles, that was a great act," I offered.

"Oh, that was nothing, only practicing my newfound skills which were taught to me by the master," he responded.

"Alright! Enough of the flattery. We need to regroup our thoughts and decide what needs doing." I said.

The sun by this stage was beginning to sink behind the trees, though there was enough light left to give us time to get home. The evening chill was beginning to set in and I was feeling peckish, having missed out on our daily meal. I was certain that Ruffles must have been feeling the same pangs, but had not mentioned a thing, so I kept my thoughts to myself.

"Since Richard and Timothy have not returned, I think it best if we wait for them here," I said instead.

"Shouldn't we go look for them?" asked Ruffles, a frown on his forehead.

"No, in so doing we may draw unwanted attention to them. Let us just make ourselves comfortable and wait beside their vehicles. They are bound to return soon." I suggested.

I gathered together a bundle of dead leaves, using my snout to nuzzle them into a neat pile. Once I was sure I had enough to make a soft bed, I curled up upon them and readied myself for sleep. When I glanced over at Ruffles I noticed that he was curled in a ball on the bare ground, his small body shivering with cold. I realised then that having been a lap dog all his life, he had no knowledge of outdoor comforts, or how to make nature provide such niceties.

"Ruffles, get over here and keep me warm!" I demanded.

He waited for no second invitation and was curled up between my legs within seconds.

"What did you see inside that cave?" he asked.

"It was a duoped in distress," I responded, "but more troubling than that, the scent was so familiar, but I cannot put a face to it. We will have to do something positive tomorrow, Ruffles, but for now, let us rest, for we will need all our strength I fear. Nestled together, using each other's body warmth, we were soon in an exhausted, dreamless sleep.

Chapter Five

The drone of an approaching vehicle wakened me. Light was just seeping into the new day, but the sun had not yet risen, and the air was chilly. We were saved from any dew thanks to the dense trees overhead, but the wind was strong today and sent a shiver through me.

"Come on Ruffles," I said, "we had better get moving and find out if this vehicle has anything to do with the cave."

Ruffles shook himself and peered around with bleary eyes.

"Is that a vehicle I can hear?" he asked, obviously having listened to not a word I said.

I glanced over to the pups' vehicle hiding place and was not surprised to find them still there. I knew that one of us would have heard something had they returned during the night.

"Yes," I replied, "and Richard and Timothy are still out there somewhere. I am very concerned for their safety, so shake yourself again and wake up!"

We moved toward the edge of the clearing and arrived just in time to see the vehicle disappearing slowly over the dune and down into the 'quarry'. We raced over to the mound having no fear of being spotted, and peered over the top carefully. The vehicle had now reached the end of the track and we watched as the furry-faced duped emerged from the cave and clambered into it. I observed the next manoeuvre with interest for I had wondered how the vehicle always exited nose first when there seemed little room for it to turn around on the narrow track. But turn it did, backwards and forwards it went, many times. With each movement it made, it turned a little more until finally the nose was facing the way it had just come.

"Quick, Ruffles, back to the cover of the trees!" I said.

We both spun around and galloped back, arriving just in time to hear the vehicle roaring over the steep incline.

"Well, now that Fur-Face has gone off in the vehicle, there should not be any duopeds left in the cave, save the one I saw lying inside of it." I said.

"Tell me more," said Ruffles.

"It was very disturbing, Ruffles," I began, "Judging by the form I saw lying there, it is probably just a pup for it was not large enough to be a full-grown duoped. I know not the purpose of it's being there, but I sense danger and foreboding. And what of our own pups? Where might they be, I wonder? There is menace in the air Ruffles, and it is a great mystery to me. Let us not dally any longer for the riddle must be solved."

The dust that had been kicked up by the vehicle had barely even settled when we were on the track leading down into the 'quarry'. The steep incline was easier to tackle on the way down than it had been coming up, and we trotted along the track, skirting the great hole toward the cave. I stopped suddenly and stood stock-still.

"What was that?" I asked having spied a movement from the corner of my eye.

Ruffles had stopped beside me and we looked up at the edge of the 'quarry' just above the cave, from where the movement had come. A moment later we spied the top of Buddy's head as she cautiously peered over the top.

"Hello!" she barked when she saw us, "Am I glad to see you!"

Richard and Timothy's heads popped up simultaneously and big grins washed over their faces immediately they spotted us.

We trotted forward as Buddy stood above the wash away we had slid down the previous evening. She carefully put her paws forward to negotiate her way down to the track. It was slippery and she went the whole way on her haunches slithering this way and that, landing in a bundle at the bottom. Richard and Timothy laughed and then made their own attempt, with much the same result.

Ruffles and I were now beside Buddy who was talking so rapidly of their experiences that it was difficult to understand what she was saying.

"Slow down Buddy," I said.

"That furry-faced duoped nearly got the pups," she managed to get out a little slower. "After you two left, he came up to examine the wash away so the pups and I dashed for cover over in the trees back there. Richard and Timothy climbed up into one of the trees just as we had found them yesterday. When the furry-faced fellow came along I bared my teeth at him and growled. He tried to get close to me but I wouldn't let him, and he eventually gave up and went away. The pups stayed in that tree all night long, afraid he may return with his friends, and I kept a close watch at its base until we heard the vehicle arriving just now," she finished in a rush, then "Did you manage to see anything inside the cave?"

"Not really," I replied, "it was too dark to see exactly what it was, but I have my suspicions. Anyway, we are about to find out."

Richard and Timothy joined us, petting us affectionately.

"Hello," said Richard, "I guess we worried about you for nothing. Although you're looking really shabby with all that dust on your fur."

"Come on then," said Timothy eagerly, "let's see what they're hiding in here."

The five of us crept stealthily forward and peered through the gloom. The air inside was stale and dank, but I still picked up the scent that I had recognised yet could not put a face to. Richard went in first with his head bent to allow him entry without bumping it on the roof of the opening, followed closely by Timothy who needed not to do the same thing, being that much shorter. They moved directly to the small body huddled beneath a grubby blanket and carefully pulled it away to reveal the form of a female pup.

"It's Kim!" they both gasped in unison.

Now it all fell into place for me. It was our neighbours' young pup and she was not looking very well. Her usually beautiful long blonde hair was dirty and matted, and the grime was caked upon her face. Her forepaws appeared to be tied behind back and she looked most uncomfortable, her head resting on the ground with nothing to pillow it. She had not stirred and I feared for her health.

"Kim," said Richard, gently shaking her shoulder.

Still no movement, but I could now hear her ragged breath and got close enough to lick her dirty face. At last she stirred with a soft moan and Richard and Timothy, one on each side of her, helped her to sit up, supporting her shoulders.

"Are you alright? What're you doing here?" asked Richard.

Kim licked her dry, cracked lips slowly as if in need of water and spoke with a raspy voice.

"I'm so thirsty," she said.

"We're going to get you out of here," said Timothy, sounding angry.

"Who are these people?" asked Richard.

"Don't know," said Kim, still with a croak and sounding groggy, "but they're horrid. I haven't had anything to eat or drink for ages, and every time they do give me some water, it is only enough to swallow a pill which puts me to sleep."

"Why are they keeping you here, Kim," asked Timothy.

"They kidnapped me," began Kim. "They came to the house and told the maid, who was looking after me, that my mom and dad had sent them to fetch me. They said they were taking me to the golf club, which is where my folks were, so we didn't think there was anything wrong. It was only when I realised that we were heading in the wrong direction that I knew something was up."

"But why, Kim?" asked Richard.

"They've got a cell phone which I heard one of them speaking into. I think he was talking to my dad 'cause he told him if he didn't pay five million dollars, he would kill me."

"How long have you been here?" asked Timothy.

"I don't know, they keep me asleep most of the time," she replied, "But I'm really scared 'cause I know they only gave my dad a week to get the money and I don't know how much time is left."

"Well, we've been spying on them for the last four days, so time is running out fast. I don't know how long you were here before we knew anything was happening," said Richard, "but we'll get you out somehow."

"You'll have to be careful guys, they've got a gun and they're really mean," she said.

I looked around the cave feeling uneasy and wishing the pups would stop talking and get into action. I was surprised to note that the cave extended quite a long way back, but it was very dark, which made it difficult to determine just how far it actually went. Buddy and Ruffles were standing at the entrance of the cave looking on with concern.

"I think I can hear the vehicle coming back," said Buddy in alarm, her ears pricked up.

Although the pups could not understand what Buddy had said, they started to move quickly at the sound of her voice and the distant rumble of an engine became more apparent.

"We won't have enough time to get her out of the quarry before they arrive. She's weak and we'll have to support her. What're we going to do?" said Timothy, sounding tense.

I nudged him with my nose trying to push him into the dark recesses of the cave where they could hide while we three dogs went for help.

"What're you doing Digby?" asked Timothy, still crouched beside Kim.

I gave him a harder nudge and he tumbled to a sitting position quite a way from Kim's side.

"Digby?" he said again.

I went over to him and nudged him yet again. He voluntarily moved backwards, slithering on his buttocks, but apparently uncertain of my motives.

"He wants you to move back into the darkness there and hide," announced Richard with sudden insight.

I nudged Timothy once more and he reached out his paw to pat me on the head.

"Good boy, Digby!" he said.

The sound of the approaching vehicle was becoming louder and I guessed it would soon be descending into the 'quarry' so I went back to Richard and nudged him really hard.

"Ok boy," said Richard, "I think we're going to have to hide back there in the dark Tim. Lie down again Kim and I'll cover you with the blanket and you'll have to pretend to be asleep as if we weren't here."

After covering Kim again, the pups moved to the back of the cave and disappeared into the darkness, whispering to each other about how surprisingly large the area was.

Once I was satisfied that they could not be seen, I turned to Buddy and Ruffles.

"We had better get out of here and find some help," I said.

The three of us took off along the track as fast as our legs could carry us.

"If that vehicle comes over the rise before we get out of here, we will be trapped," I said feeling a little apprehensive.

"I noticed a smaller inlet at the end of the track close to where we hid the last time," announced Ruffles proudly, "I don't know if we'll all fit into it, but it might be worth a try."

"Well done dog," said I "get a move on then!"

As we got to the steep incline I could hear the vehicle bearing down on us, for it must have been getting close. We went to the end of the track where it tapered and sure enough, there was indeed an inlet. I had not noticed it before, probably because I was still in a bit of a stupor from the bang on the head I had received.

Ruffles went in first, but the opening was too narrow for Buddy's broad shoulders to squeeze through.

"Carry on, Digby," she offered, "I'll just stand outside; I don't think they'll see me."

I pushed my way in beside Ruffles; it was a tight fit. Buddy had just moved into position when the nose of the vehicle came over the top and edged its way down and around onto the track.

"Let's head for the hills," shouted Buddy jovially, and we were out of the 'quarry' and in behind the tree line in record-breaking time.

* * * * * * * * * * * * * * * * * *

We were all aware of the urgency of our mission, but the hunger pangs were becoming even more compelling, as I thought we would be unable to accomplish much without sustenance. We headed directly for Fred and Wilma, who appeared to be well fed and therefore, I reasoned, would have ample food that we might scrounge.

The sun had risen by now, but was weak and provided little warmth to the wintry air. We made good time, but the Labradors were not standing at their gate when we arrived. They rushed around from the back of the house, however, immediately upon hearing our calls.

"Hello friends," said Fred, a delightful smile on his good-natured face.

"Hi," replied Ruffles, "you wouldn't have any food for us would you?"

"We've just finished our meal," said Wilma hanging her head in shame.

"I'm afraid we both have very healthy appetites," said Fred, "we never leave anything in our bowls. In fact we always have a race to see who can finish first."

"Not a problem," offered Buddy, "I'm sure there will be enough for the three of us when we get back to my place."

We discussed the events of the previous day and this early morning, Ruffles constantly interrupting to get his version heard.

"It sounds like you could do with some help," said Fred, "you three wouldn't be able to take on three large duopeds alone."

"Is your small gate open today?" I asked.

"I'm afraid not," replied Wilma, "I had a wander along there earlier."

"I would like to examine it if you wouldn't mind," I said.

"Sure thing," said Fred, as they both padded off along the inside of the wall toward the small duoped gate.

Buddy, Ruffles and I trotted along the outside of the wall and we all met again with the gate separating us. I investigated the latch and found a solution immediately.

"We will be back as quickly as possible," I said to Fred and Wilma, and then to Buddy and Ruffles, "come along you two, we had better find some food before we all expire."

When we arrived at Buddy's 'place', entering through the dilapidated fence at the rear of the garden, her bowl of food was indeed plentiful. Once she had eaten her fill there was ample left for Ruffles and I, neither of us being big eaters. We all swallowed vast amounts of water for we were unsure when another opportunity would arise, and left again using the same route.

Once we were back on the road in front of Buddy's garden we trotted over to Jamie's gate where she was waiting impatiently.

"Where have you all been?" she asked, apparently distressed over our long absence.

We related our tales to which she listened intently.

"We will need your assistance Jamie, if you are willing to come along," I said.

"I wouldn't miss it for the world," she replied, "but I've never attempted jumping this gate, so I don't know if I can do it."

"Well, there is no better time to try," I offered, then remembering a duoped saying, "there's no time like the present. But before you do," I continued, "I need to ask you a great favour. Those young pups will all be hungry and will need their strength. It is an awful thing to ask I know, but if you still have your skills, could you steal some food for them?"

Jamie looked uncertainly from one to the other of us, took a deep breath and turned around, walking away in a rather dejected manner. She disappeared into the house and came back moments later with a packet in her mouth. She put it gently on the ground and pushed it beneath the gate with her nose.

"This is the lunch mother has prepared for father to take to work. I'll be in big bad trouble when they discover it missing," she said.

Then without further ado she turned and walked away from us again. When she reached a distance she considered a long enough run-up, she stopped, turned and stared at the gate for a long time, evidently sizing it up. With a look of deep concentration on her face, she took two great inhalations of breath and charged at the gate. At what appeared to be just the right moment she soared into the air, her forelegs rising easily over the top pole of the gate, but her hind legs were dragging low behind her. Both back legs caught the gate and she tumbled ungracefully to the ground, landing painfully outside the garden. A great whoosh of air escaped her as her huge body slammed into the compacted driveway.

I rushed over to her, Buddy and Ruffles seemingly rooted to the ground.

"Jamie!" I called, "are you alright?"

There was no response, as she lay motionless in a tangled heap. "Jamie!" I shouted.

Still no response.

I nudged her with my nose and then prodded her chest hard with my forepaw. Suddenly she took in a deep gulp of air and lifted her great head.

The other two dashed across, Ruffles' tail wagging gleefully.

"We thought we'd lost you Jamie, are you Ok?" he asked.

She struggled to a sitting position, gasping for more air, apparently winded from the fall, with an expression of pain across her face.

"I'll be alright," she gasped, "but my hind legs are aching."

I examined them cautiously, not wanting to hurt her any more than she already was. There appeared to be no breaks.

"I am hoping you are just bruised, Jamie," I consoled, "rest a little while."

The four of us sat together companionably waiting for Jamie to regain her breath, and hopefully, for the pain to subside. After what seemed an eternity, Jamie stood up unsteadily on her four paws and gingerly took a few steps forward. She was obviously still in agony, but managed to speak without gasping.

"I'll be fine," she said, "they're just a little stiff I think."

"Do you think you will be able to run?" I asked delicately.

"The more exercise I do, the better they'll get I'm sure. I know if I just sit around they'll get stiffer and stiffer," she replied.

So we trotted off gently down the road towards Snoopy's home. There was no sign of him or his friend Pepi, so we all called out together.

"I think they've gone a hunting!" said Ruffles with humour in his voice and indicating the gate, which was slightly ajar.

Oscar appeared at his fence, his forepaws and ugly little snout dirty from digging.

"'Morning," he greeted cheerfully, "they've taken off for their morning run, but they'll be back soon enough. What have you lot been up to then? And what have you got in that packet," he asked, "it smells great!"

"It is food for no dog, Oscar, but for the young pups we have told you of," said I.

After introducing Buddy and Jamie we related our stories yet again, and at the conclusion, Oscar asked if he could come along and participate in our quest to rescue the pups.

"I think the more dog presence we have the better it will be," I agreed, "but we will have to wait for Snoopy and Pepi, for we will need their assistance too."

Oscar scrambled out through the hole he had dug beneath the fence and it was not long after this that Snoopy and Pepi returned, a little out of breath, but with happy faces. We reported our activities in shorter form, without having to contend with Ruffles' constant interruptions, as he had seemingly become bored with the telling of it. So now there were seven of us in greatly varying sizes and shapes, and we padded along the road back toward Fred and Wilma's home.

We went immediately to the small duoped gate upon our arrival.

"Could you two open this gate?" I asked Snoopy and Pepi.

"Not a problem," replied Snoopy after inspecting the latch.

He jumped up standing on his hind legs, his forepaws resting not on the gate as I had expected, but against the side post. He placed his snout beneath the latch and flicked it up. Pepi quickly pushed the gate inwards, but it was going in the wrong direction and bounced back on its hinges, swinging hard towards us. We all skipped out of the way and then barked our delight at this clever pair.

Fred and Wilma rushed out from behind the wall having heard all the excitement and looked in astonishment at the open gate.

"That's so cool! How did you manage it?" asked Fred in wonderment.

"Top secret," said Snoopy with a smile on his jolly face, "how do you do, I'm Snoopy, this is my friend Pepi, and my neighbour Oscar."

"And I'm Jamie," said Jamie, feeling a little left out.

"Pleased to meet you all," responded Fred and Wilma simultaneously.

"Before we move on Fred, would it be possible for you to carry some water to the pups? They will be in dire need of a drink by the time we get to them, and perhaps since Wilma has such a soft mouth, she could carry the food that we have brought," I suggested.

"I surely can, but you'll have to keep an eye on Wilma or she'll eat that food," replied Fred with a grin on his face.

I followed Fred back into the garden and as he scouted around for a container, I strolled across to the large clear pond for a drink myself. He returned with a small pail hanging from his mouth and dropped it into the water, not letting go of the paw hold. I watched in amazement as the pail slowly filled and Fred lifted it out. It put a bit of strain on his strong neck and I wondered if he would manage to carry it all the way to the 'quarry'. We went back to the others, Fred having difficulty keeping the water from slopping over the side of the pail.

Wilma took charge of the food, carrying it gently in her mouth as Labradors are known to do, and we were back on the road again. The going was slow and, regrettably, by the time we reached our destination, Fred's pail was all but empty. Thankfully though, Wilma had not eaten any of the food.

Chapter Six

We were all lined up along the dune, peering over the top, nine very different heads in a row. Down below, parked outside the cave, was the vehicle. We all watched with interest, for there seemed to be a great deal of activity, with articles of various sizes and shapes being transferred from the cave to the vehicle. I had not noticed anything else in that cave besides young Kim, which must mean that whatever it was they were moving had been hidden in the recesses. Suddenly an alarm bell rang inside my head.

"The pups!" I said in panic, "they are bound to find the pups."

Eight heads turned to look at me, each with their own individual look of dread upon their faces.

As we watched, the two duopeds we had met before emerged from the cave, propelling in front of them, Richard and Timothy. Our worst fears had unfolded before our eyes. It seemed that the pups had their paws tied behind their backs for they offered no resistance. The duoped with the potbelly and some cloth wrapped around his right forelimb, shoved Richard roughly and he stumbled forward. Being unable to put out his paws to save himself, he fell to the earth and rolled dangerously close to the edge of the great pit. Every dog was ready to charge.

"Wait!" I said, trying to think of what we could do, "if we all charge down there now, we could spoil their chances of rescue."

Potbelly bent over and roughly hauled Richard up from the ground, driving him again toward the vehicle. He opened the rear door and pushed Richard in, slamming it shut immediately, he was inside. Fur-Face, in the mean time, was dealing with Timothy in a kindlier fashion, though the end result was the same.

A giant of a duoped came forth from the opening of the cave carrying Kim, still wrapped in the soiled blanket and apparently asleep once again. Kim looked diminutive by comparison and frail indeed. This giant, who wore a great mop of fur atop his head, must have been the one who always drove the vehicle, and that would explain the reason for us never having seen him before now.

Kim was placed in the back seat of the vehicle together with Richard and Timothy. Fur-Face clambered in beside them and the other two got into the front seat. The engine started and the vehicle began it's manoeuvres to turn around.

"We are going to have to follow that vehicle. We cannot let it out of our sight or we will lose the pups for certain," I said.

"But it's hard enough keeping up with the pups when they're on their bi-wheeled vehicles, we'll never manage to follow a quadruwheeled vehicle," responded Ruffles.

"How are your legs doing Jamie?" I asked, "you have the longest by far and so stand a better chance of maintaining great speeds than do the rest of us."

"The pain is only slight now, I'm sure I can do it," she replied gallantly.

The vehicle had by now turned around and was moving towards us, so we all ducked our heads from view.

"Right, here is the plan," I began, "we have no idea which direction the vehicle will take, so Jamie will follow as best she can and we will all do our utmost to keep up with her. Failing that we can at least follow her scent should we lose sight of her. Remember, there is safety in numbers, so we must try to stay as close together as possible. A motley army of dogs we may appear, but defeat our enemy we shall!" I finished valiantly.

The vehicle suddenly thundered up out of the 'quarry', clouds of dust billowing out from beneath it. It hurtled into the air and came down hard upon its wheels, flattening the base of the tyres momentarily. We had never been as close to it as this before and were able to see the occupants being bounced out of their seats, almost hitting their heads on the roof.

The roar of the motor eased slightly and the vehicle slowed down. Instead of taking the track leading away from the 'quarry', it turned sharply to the right along an evidently old and unused track running through the bush. I considered this a good omen as I guessed it would mean that the vehicle would be unable to increase its speed too greatly.

We all accelerated into action together like the beginning of a race. Fred left his almost empty pail behind, but Wilma dutifully picked up her parcel of food for the pups. It was not too long before the pack began to separate, the fitter ones taking the lead, the fatter ones pulling up the rear.

The vehicle bounced and bumped along the rutted trail, spewing out dust in its wake, but maintained a cautious speed, which fortunately allowed Jamie and Buddy to keep close behind. I began to hang back so that I could encourage the stragglers to persevere with their struggle. The three small poodles and Snoopy were in the middle of the pack, but fairly well spread out, while Fred and Wilma laboured to make headway some distance at the back.

I was running alongside the smaller dogs, my own flanks beginning to heave from the effort. Jamie and Buddy had gone out of sight, but I was not worried, for I knew that we would track them down easily enough. I glanced over my shoulder periodically to keep an eye on the Labradors, who were falling further and further behind us.

"I am going to wait for Fred and Wilma," I called in between panting, "They seem to be battling a little."

The others were too exhausted to reply but nodded their agreement to me and pressed on. I waited in the middle of the trail, regaining my breath, and watched, as Fred and Wilma got gradually closer, but at a slower and slower pace.

Finally, when they reached me, Wilma collapsed, her forelegs outstretched. She carefully placed the food package atop her forepaws, her flanks swelling and subsiding in an unhealthy pattern. Her kind eyes were glazed, the whites showing, and her tongue hung out of the side of her mouth flapping up and down as she gasped for breath. Her courage tugged at my heartstrings. She was quite unable to speak, but managed a faint smile. I smiled back at her and glanced across at Fred.

His condition was not as pronounced as Wilma's, but he, too, was in a state of disorder. It was quite apparent that these two got little or no exercise, and their obesity was not in their favour. He too had collapsed, his forepaws crossed over each other in a more relaxed pose. His eyes were more alert too, though his flanks heaved and his tongue hung out.

"I wish now I'd brought that little bit of water," he gasped, a mischievous grin on his face.

"We will take it a bit slower from here on," I said, feeling very worried for Wilma's well being, "there will be no difficulty tracking their spoor and I will stay with you to ensure that you are both alright."

"You're very sweet and thoughtful, Digby," said Wilma weakly.

I gave the Labradors a little more time to recover and then persuaded them to make a move. They both rose laboriously to their four paws, flinching, but saying not a word in argument, and Wilma carefully retrieved her burden. We began by walking, but with some encouragement from me, they were able to manage a slow trot. I was becoming anxious as to the distance we would have to travel. There was no sign of the other dogs and the dust had long since settled. Eventually I decided that I would hasten on ahead to see how much further we would need to go, and left Fred and Wilma trotting almost comfortably along the trail behind me.

I moved quickly, stopping periodically to ensure that I had not lost the scent, but it was easy enough following the tyre tracks as they were the only ones that had passed through this way for many a long year. As I rounded a corner I spied the vehicle through the trees and stopped abruptly. I could not see the other dogs, though could sense their presence, and left the trail, moving through the trees stealthily. The vehicle was parked outside a very broken-down wooden shack and I crept nearer, keeping close to the ground.

Then I saw my newfound friends, huddled together, apparently having a conference, some distance to the left of the shack partially hidden in the trees, so I sneaked up and joined them.

"Is every dog alright?" I asked.

Buddy, who had her back to me, almost jumped out of her coat.

"Where're Fred and Wilma?" asked Ruffles.

"They are having difficulty due to their excessive weight," I answered, "but I shall go back to direct them shortly. Have you discovered anything?"

71

"Oh, yes," said Jamie, "we know why they left the cave in such a hurry. It seems that the giant had overheard a conversation in town about the cell phone they've been using."

"That's right," said Ruffles, back to his usual interfering self, unable to resist telling the story himself. "He told the others that the cops had traced the number, found it was a stolen phone, and were now trying to pinpoint its location through the signal, so he instructed Fur-Face to switch it off," he concluded excitedly.

"Did you actually understand all that you have just told me?" I asked, once again astonished by Ruffles' intelligence.

"No," he replied, "I don't understand any of it but that's what the giant said."

"Ok, well done Ruffles, so what happened next?" I asked.

Buddy opened her mouth to speak, but Ruffles interrupted yet again.

"They were talking about Richard and Timothy," continued Ruffles, "they say they're going to have to shoot them 'cause they'll be able to recognise them. We have to get them out of there, Digby, and quickly!"

"Yes, and so we shall!" I declared, feeling angrier than I had ever felt in all of my long life. "Let me go and find the Labradors, I shall be back soon. Keep a keen eye on that shack in my absence. Do anything you have to do to keep those pups alive until I get back."

I crept back the way I had come and when I reached the corner I could see Fred and Wilma not too far back down the trail. Wilma was still dutifully carrying the food package, and I wondered if it would be fit for the pups to eat by the time they received it. I felt a swell of pride at my little dog army and their tremendous courage.

"Well done you two, come this way, I have found the others," I said, and they followed obediently.

Once we were all together again, hidden beneath the trees, I called another meeting to discuss our strategy, for our assignment was already clear.

"We have to get inside that shack, but the door appears firmly closed. Does any dog have an idea?" I asked.

"Fur-Face seems to like dogs," began Buddy, "maybe if Pepi, being the cutest by far, went and scratched on the door, he might open it for him. Then we could all rush in and attack."

"What if someone other than Fur-Face opens the door?" asked Ruffles.

"Duopeds seem to think that ugly dogs are cute, so maybe Oscar should be the one to do that," suggested Snoopy, that appealing grin on his face.

Oscar rolled his eyes to the sky, but could not hide the amusement in them. What a character he was turning out to be, I thought.

"Has any dog had a look at the latch holding that door closed?" I asked, thinking that perhaps Snoopy and Pepi could work their magic on it.

"There's no latch on the outside of the door," offered Jamie, "it seems to be secured on the inside."

"What about the windows?" I asked.

"The transparent material is missing, but the windows are too high in the walls for the smaller dogs to get through," answered Buddy.

"Has any dog been around the back of the shack? It looks very dilapidated, so perhaps we could break through some loosened boards?" I suggested.

None of my dog soldiers had visited that area, so Oscar volunteered to take a look and disappeared into the undergrowth quietly.

He was back after a short interval and reported that the shack was boarded up too tightly for any dog to get through. We had now run out of options, and sat silently pondering our problem. Suddenly Fred stood on his four paws, clearing his throat.

"Ahem! The idea of Pepi scratching on the door is workable," he suggested, "but I think he is too small, no offence intended Pepi. What we need is a large dog, heavy enough to bulldoze his or her way through, ensuring that the door is opened wide enough for the rest of us to rush in behind."

"Very good idea!" I congratulated, "do we have any volunteers?"

"Buddy would be the ideal choice," suggested Snoopy.

"Once again, there is no offence intended, but Buddy's not a particularly appealing dog to duopeds. Her looks are too fearsome. I was actually thinking of myself," said Fred, eyes alert and ready to do battle.

"Alright then," I said, "let us make our plans, and remember, we have only one chance at this."

* *

Fred and Wilma stood side by side outside the door to the shack, tails wagging so hard that their bottoms were waving from side to side. Their ears pricked up and eyes bright, they looked a perfect picture of affectionate dogs. Fred barked his 'hello' in the friendliest voice I have ever heard him use.

Goliath opened the door enough to allow him to put his head through, and peered at the Labradors quizzically. The tail wagging increased in speed and Fred gave another bark, then together they pushed their way through the door, forcing Goliath to stagger back into the shack. Pepi and Oscar squeezed in beneath the Labradors bellies unseen by the duopeds. It all happened so quickly from then on.

Snoopy and Ruffles, who were standing on one side of the door out of view from the inside of the shack, rushed around the corner and in through the door so rapidly, that the duopeds barely noticed them in the confusion. Buddy, who had been standing on the other side of the door, hurtled through directly behind the smaller dogs. Shock registered upon the faces of all duopeds, the pups included, as the tiny one-roomed shack filled up with dogs.

At precisely the same moment that Buddy entered through the door, Jamie and I launched ourselves through the window, flank to flank. We soared through the air, unhampered due to the lack of transparent material in the window frame. Jamie landed heavily upon the single table, which collapsed under her weight, and I tumbled down atop one of the chairs, turning it over.

Potbelly reached for the gun, which had fallen to the floor in the commotion, and Buddy leapt at him, sailing over the smaller dogs and landing squarely upon his bent back, knocking him down with a thunderous crash. The gun thumped away across the wooden floor and stopped just short of Richard's hind paws. As Potbelly tried to get to his hind paws, Buddy lunged forward again, this time bowling him over onto his back. She immediately went for his throat, pinning him to the floor where he stayed, too afraid to move now, for each time he had tried, Buddy pressed harder with those powerful jaws.

At the same time, Jamie had regained her paws and laid into Goliath with a similar attack. He was such a huge duoped, however, that she was unable to contain him on her own, so Wilma moved in to help, throwing herself upon his upturned belly and using her sheer weight to pin him down, while Jamie placed her great jaws around his throat.

In the mean time, Pepi, Oscar, Ruffles and Snoopy were doing their best to get Fur-Face to the floor, but he was swiping and kicking at them constantly. At least twice I saw Pepi flying through the air, but he was back in a flash, nipping his ankles and successfully drawing blood. Oscar, Ruffles and Snoopy had the trousers of the other hind limb; pulling so hard that Fur-Face almost did the splits before finally collapsing. Now that they had him where they wanted him, Snoopy and Ruffles went for the throat and the other two little ones sat upon his chest snarling fiercely.

I spied a movement from Potbelly, and saw his paw reaching out for the gun only inches away. Fred was closer than I, and more adept at carrying objects in his mouth, so I called out to him urgently to retrieve the weapon as I hurled myself across the room to assist. Fred launched himself at Potbelly, who had grasped the gun in his uninjured paw, and sunk his teeth savagely into the duoped's forelimb, snarling and growling ferociously. Potbelly howled in pain and the weapon dropped from his paw. As the gun clattered to the floor it went off with a thunderous roar, and for a number of seconds, we were all stunned.

Finally, as the gun smoke dissipated, my ears still humming, Potbelly cried out in pain.

"He's been shot, Digby," called Timothy.

I immediately advised Fred and Buddy to release him, for I felt certain that he would be unable to cause any further trouble for the time being. It was then that I noticed blood seeping from his hind limb, not far up from his huge paw. He knew not which part of his anatomy to grasp for he must have pain in both of his forelimbs, his throat and now his hind limb. I ignored him, considering that he had got no more than he deserved, and turned to Buddy.

"Are you Ok?" I asked Fred and Buddy, very concerned, for I thought the shock of the gunshot might have shaken them a little.

Buddy shook her head, still dazed.

"What happened?" she asked.

Fred was staring at the wall, a blank expression on his face. I went closer to him and licked his face in an attempt to revive him. He shuddered and then shook himself.

"Wow!" he said, "that was quite something."

Satisfied that they were both all right, I glanced around the room to evaluate the impact of this latest event upon the others.

Wilma and Jamie still had Goliath pinned to the floor, Jamie letting out a low growl every now and then to warn him that should he try anything foolish, she would not hesitate to puncture the skin of his throat. The others were successfully holding down Fur-Face, who seemed to be offering no resistance. The situation was at last under the control of the dog army!

I turned to the pups, content that Fred and Buddy would keep an eye on Potbelly, and wondered how we were going to get the tethers off from around Richard and Timothy's paws. Kim was lodged between them, still sleeping, so they would be unable to undo the ropes for each other. I thought she must be drugged deeply for her not to waken with the clamour that had been going on. I also wondered how we were going to get her out of the shack in the state she was in, for I knew the pups would be unable to carry her.

Chapter Seven

A peaceful quiet had descended upon the occupants of the shack as I sat at the open door thinking of the next step to take. The captives and their captors were in the same positions, silently enduring their respective appointments. The only sounds to be heard were the birds singing in the trees outside and the occasional groan from Potbelly. Even the pups sat quietly, no doubt contemplating their next move.

I was confused, and having difficulty arriving at a solution to my dilemma. An idea of using Pepi's small sharp teeth to gnaw through the ropes binding the paws of the pups ran through my head, but the chances of hurting them were too great. There was no possibility of using the weapon, lying discarded on the floor, to keep one of the duopeds in line while he untied the ropes. The problem seemed insurmountable.

As my mind wandered from one possible answer to another, a sound infiltrated my thoughts. It took a while before I realised that it was the purr of an engine I could hear.

I leapt to my paws, ears pricked to listen more closely and sure enough, it was a vehicle drawing closer.

"At last!" I thought, "the answer to my deliberations."

I watched as a rather flashy red vehicle turned the corner and headed directly for the shack. There was only one duoped that I could see and he wore a cap, which I thought might indicate that he was a policeman, so I wagged my pompom happily.

The vehicle drew to an abrupt halt in a cloud of dust and the duoped immediately flung the door open and stepped out. He marched toward the shack with a determined stride and I watched in horror as he withdrew a gun from his side pocket.

"Oh no," I groaned, "not another one."

"What the devil's going on here," he boomed, removing his cap and revealing a totally bald head.

I spun around and rushed back through the door.

"Release your captives, dogs!" I shouted urgently, "We have an unfriendly newcomer and those you are holding are not worth dying for."

My dog army withdrew immediately and moved protectively toward the pups as the newcomer entered the shack in a flurry, waving his weapon around the room ominously. Goliath and Fur-Face were cautiously rising to a sitting position, while Potbelly remained huddled in the corner, unable to lick his wounds.

"Get to your feet!" demanded the newcomer, "the cops are close on our tail so we'd better get out of here pretty quick."

"What're we gonna do with this lot?" asked Goliath.

"We'll take the kid, but leave the rest, they can't do us any harm," replied the bald one.

"Those two boys can identify us," said Goliath, threateningly.

"The last thing we want is dead bodies on our hands," declared Baldy, "besides we
have no time and we'll be long gone across the Botswana border before anybody finds them. That vehicle out front, is it stolen?"

"'Course it is," replied Goliath.

"Have you changed the number plates?" questioned Baldy.

"What do you take me for?" responded Goliath irritably, "I'm no idiot you know. It's had a new paint job and number plates."

"Good! Then we'll use that. They'll have traced mine by now and be looking for it. Now let's get out of here!" shouted Baldy.

"Give him a hand," said Goliath to Fur-Face; indicating Potbelly, "I'll get the girl."

Fur-Face helped Potbelly to his only uninjured hind paw and acted as a crutch for him while he hopped toward the door. Goliath retrieved the gun and then pushed his way through my motley army, dragged Kim to her paws, slinging her over his shoulder, then marched out after Fur-Face, pulling the door shut with a loud bang behind him.

We all looked at each other and then at the pups, not certain what to do next. We heard the four doors of the vehicle slamming shut, the engine roaring into life, and then listened to the drone rapidly disappearing into the distance.

"We have to get that door open," I said suddenly, "Snoopy, can you work your magic on that latch?"

"The door opens the wrong way, Digby, I need another dog on the other side of it," he replied with a downcast expression on his face.

I noticed that the pups had worked themselves into a position where they were back to back, and were busy on the ropes around their paws. Without further ado, I leapt through the window and positioned myself outside the door.

"Let me know when you are ready, Snoopy," I said through the wood.

"Now!" said Snoopy after a brief interval.

I pressed both of my forepaws against the door and it swung open swiftly, knocking Snoopy out of the way. I padded across the room to the pups and sat down to watch the progress they were making with the ropes. It was interminably slow, so I called Pepi and asked if he could assist.

"I don't know," he said, "but I'll sure give it a try."

Fred had been sniffing around under the window and unexpectedly let out a howl of delight. He turned to face us, grinning as he displayed a small knife between his jaws.

"Well done, Fred," I said.

He trotted across to the pups and carefully placed the knife into one of their paws. Moments later they were free and had rushed to the open door.

Outside, parked in the same place that the bald one had left it, was the flashy red vehicle. Richard and Timothy made straight for it and opened the front door. My bedraggled army trotted along behind them and peered in through the open door from different levels. That was when I noticed that Wilma was not among the pack and I glanced over my shoulder to see where she had gone. I was just in time to observe her disappear into the undergrowth, only to return a few moments later with something clutched delicately in her mouth.

I barked my delight when I realised what it was she was carrying.

"You are a treasure, Wilma, I had completely forgotten that," I congratulated her.

She approached at a trot, tail wagging shyly, and stopped in front of the pups, carefully placing the food package on the ground in front of their hind paws.

"What's this?" asked Richard as he bent to pick it up.

"They've brought us some food!" said Timothy joyously, watching Richard opening the package.

The pups wolfed down the food in a matter of minutes, evidently starving.

The sun was by now high in the sky and the chill had gone out of the air, there was not a cloud in sight. The pups had finished their food, and immediately turned their attention once again to the vehicle.

"A BMW, wow!" said Richard.

"It's automatic," observed Timothy.

"Whatever that might mean," I said to my friends.

"Just as well," said Richard, "or I wouldn't be able to reach the pedals to change gear."

Timothy opened the rear door and motioned for us to get in. I looked at my dog soldiers questioningly, wondering if this were a good idea. Then I indicated that they should all embark ahead of me. Ruffles, Pepi and Oscar leapt in first and went directly to the back shelf behind the seat, up against the rear window. Fred and Wilma were next and sat themselves down upon the back seat, taking up more than half of it between them. Buddy and Jamie clambered in and squashed up beside the Labradors, leaving no room for another dog.

"Ok," said Timothy, "you two will have to come in the front with us."

He moved around to the other side of the vehicle and opened the front door. I allowed Snoopy to hop in before me and followed immediately. Timothy climbed in beside us as Richard entered from the other side and placed himself behind the steering wheel. A strange sight we must have been indeed.

Richard turned the key and the engine roared into life.

"My legs are still a little too short," said Richard, who could barely see over the top of the dashboard.

"Sit on the edge of the seat," suggested Timothy.

Richard moved forward, tucking his left hind leg under the seat and extending his right as far as it could reach.

"Ok, Here goes!" he said, as he moved the gear stick into position and the vehicle shot forward alarmingly fast.

"Slow down!" said Timothy.

"I can't reach the break pedal," said Richard.

However, he had already taken his foot off the accelerator and the vehicle was slowing down automatically. I wondered if this was what was meant by "automatic".

Richard steered the vehicle in the opposite direction to the one we had come in on, along another unused trail.

"Why are you going this way?" asked Timothy.

"Look at the tracks," said Richard, "this is the way they went in the four by four."

A question mark hung over my head yet again.

Timothy sat up straight and leaned forward to see over the bonnet.

"Oh, yes, I see them," he said.

We bumped along the track slowly as Richard depressed the pedal gently, evidently having got the feel of it now. The trail wound in between the trees and around great boulders. It was rutted and covered with smaller stones, making the going rough, but Richard held the wheel in his strong paws, an expression of deep concentration upon his youthful face.

As we rounded a corner, the vehicle unexpectedly began to increase speed as it descended a steep slope.

"I can't reach the brake," said Richard again, a little panic in his voice.

Sitting in the front seat I could see a riverbed rushing toward us. There was only a trickle of water, but mountainous rocks covered the waterway and I sensed impending doom.

Timothy leaned forward clutching the dash, apparently also aware of imminent disaster, but said nothing. Richard fought with the steering wheel, which kicked and bucked under his grip, and I could see that he was fast losing control. The vehicle sped up as it gained momentum, fairly hurtling toward the watercourse now.

Richard eased off the front of the seat, hanging from the steering wheel with his paws, and finally managed to reach the brake pedal.

He depressed it as hard as he could, but he had taken the action too late. The vehicle slowed marginally, then bounced over a large rock, scraping the underside noisily and veering off the track. The screeching sound of branches against metal made my teeth go on edge as the vehicle bumped and jostled through the bushes and trees.

Richard had lost control completely now and clung to the steering wheel more for support than in an attempt to direct the vehicle. It had at least slowed considerably due to the continuous bouncing and so when the final crunch came, it was not as terrible as it could have been. It landed virtually in the riverbed, its nose crunched against a huge boulder, with a great grinding coming from the underside, steam belching from under the bonnet. We were all flung forward; the three little dogs on the rear shelf were tossed so hard that they landed atop the four sitting on the back seat, in a tangled mess of canine limbs, thrashing and snarling at each other. Snoopy, who had been sitting beside me, was thrown against the dash painfully, smashing his nose, and let out a yelp. Being taller, the bashing I took from the dash was only against my chest and therefore not so hurtful. Richard and Timothy were clutching the steering wheel and dash respectively, and so escaped any serious injury.

When the vehicle finally came to a rasping halt, pandemonium erupted with the seven dogs in the rear seat fighting to recover their pawing. Timothy regained his composure first and threw open the door, leaping out to open the back door so that the dogs could extricate themselves. It was one of the funniest sights I had ever seen, for they tumbled out, one atop the other, still grumbling unhappily.

Richard scrambled out from under the steering wheel, apparently unhurt, and opened his door. I followed him out of the vehicle and so was on the other side from the rest of the pack, Snoopy having exited through Timothy's door after his tumble had changed his position, but I could still hear those dogs bickering. Oscar was the first to notice it, and put an instant stop to the proceedings.

"Water!" he shouted, and rushed over to the trickle running through the rocks.

Every dog and the pups followed suit, and the only sound that could be heard was the splashing of water and laughter from the pups.

Fred and Wilma

All the discomfort and aches were forgotten as we romped around, splashing each other playfully. Oh, and how beautiful that liquid tasted, clear and cold, the most refreshing drink I had ever had.

Fred and Wilma looked as though they had been born to the water for they rolled around in it, rollicking like puppies. Richard and Timothy joined in their fun, thoroughly enjoying the Labradors. Fred, being typical of his breed, continuously tried to save Timothy whenever he strayed into deeper water, taking his paw into his mouth and tugging him gently to the edge. Finally, all of them exhausted, Fred, Wilma and the pups dragged themselves out of the stream and collapsed, panting heavily, onto a sandbank at the side. The remainder of the pack, myself included, continued for some time after that, enjoying the company, and the water, to the full.

* * * * * * * * * * * * * * * * * * * *

Eventually, when we had all regained our breath and taken our fill of that glorious liquid, Richard and Timothy got to their paws.

"Time to move on," announced Richard.

"It doesn't look like we're going to be able to use that car again," observed Timothy.

"No," conceded Richard, "I think I trashed it real good. Anyway, we've got their tracks to follow, and we have to catch up with them to save Kim, so let's get moving!"

With that, my small army and the pups scrambled up the other side of the steep riverbed and continued along the trail. I noticed that Buddy was having difficulty with her hind legs and presumed that her arthritis was playing up again. Obviously, the romping in the water and then the prolonged rest afterwards had set if off.

The going was rough under paw, for besides the rutted track, there were numerous stones of varying sizes. This made following the spoor of the vehicle difficult too, and it was only by the disturbed stones that we were able to confirm that the vehicle had in fact passed this way. However, even without these signs, we knew that it could have gone no other way, for the dense bush would not have allowed the passage of any vehicle.

Calculating the position of the sun, I judged that midday had come and gone, but there would still be several hours of light left to us. The track wound back and forth, almost making a zigzag effect, and probably doubling our distance. Then as we rounded a corner, we came unexpectedly across the vehicle that the duopeds had escaped in. It was lying upon its side, its great wheels unmoving.

"Get down!" said Richard quietly, waving his paw at us as he himself crouched behind a tree, Timothy at his side.

85

"Do you think they're still in there?" asked Timothy.

"Don't know. Don't think so, but we'd better go in carefully anyway. We must be some time behind them by now," replied Richard.

He crept silently toward the vehicle, Timothy close to his heels.

"Stay there, dogs," instructed Timothy.

Not one of my motley army obeyed, but followed soundlessly behind the pups, treading carefully upon the stones so as not to dislodge them.

The pups arrived first and peered in through the windscreen.

"There's nobody here," said Richard.

"I wonder which way they went?" said Timothy.

Without need of instruction, the dogs scattered, sniffing the ground for scent of the duopeds.

"They can't be moving very fast," said Richard, looking around, "they've got fatso who's been shot in the foot and Kim is probably still sound asleep. I hope she didn't get hurt in this."

"What do you think happened?" asked Timothy.

"Probably came around that corner too fast and lost control," replied Richard.

"This way!" I called to the others, having picked up the scent further up the trail going off into the bush to the left. I do not think that the pups understood my words, but they followed the rest of the pack as they darted across to me, putting their noses to the ground.

"I think Richard is quite right. I do not think that the duopeds will be moving all that rapidly. Follow me, and keep your wits about you, we do not want to lose their trail," I said.

The bush was thick and the spoor on the ground was almost invisible, but the duopeds had trampled the undergrowth, making it easy to follow, and their scent was still strong, so we made steady progress. After some time we arrived at a field planted with luscious green foliage.

"Winter wheat," announced Richard.

"How d'you know its wheat?" asked Timothy.

"Because it's winter," replied Richard logically.

Following the trail was easier going through the wheat for the duopeds had carelessly trampled a path. The going was also more comfortable under paw with the ground soft and moist.

"We must be on someone's farm," observed Richard.

"Where d'you think they're headed?" asked Timothy.

"Probably to the farm house to steal another car," suggested Richard.

Sure enough, when we arrived at the other end of the field, the farmhouse was visible in the distance. Great tall trees surrounded it with luxurious green grass, cropped short. We were all crouched down in the wheat and I was formulating a plan.

"Gather around friends," I said to the dogs, and they all did as they were told, sitting before me, patiently awaiting my next command.

"Pepi, you are the smallest and therefore the least likely to be seen. Would you volunteer to go and take a look? If Jamie or Buddy were to go, they may arouse other dogs in the area," I said.

"Sure thing," replied Pepi, and scampered off in the direction of the farmhouse.

Richard and Timothy had been watching us curiously, but never said a word.

Whilst we awaited Pepi's return, we sat listening to the pups, sitting cross

legged among the wheat, discussing how they would perform the great rescue.

"First, we'll have to find out if there is anyone else in the house," began Richard, "then we'll have to see where they all are. At least we know how many they are."

"We can use the dogs, they seem to know exactly what to do," responded Timothy.

"We'll check out the situation through the windows, and then we must count the number of doors leading outside so we can find the best way in. Once we're inside, we'll have to get those guns off them. They have two, now. Like you say, the dogs seem to know what to do, so hopefully they'll give us a hand there," said Richard.

"We need something to tie them up with once we've got them, then we can phone the police," suggested Timothy.

"There's a barn over there," said Richard, pointing to the left of the farmhouse, "maybe there's some rope in there."

"I wonder why that little poodle went off like that? D'you think he was sent out as a scout?" asked Timothy.

"Don't know," said Richard, "but we'll wait 'till he gets back anyway."

As they talked I realised that any plans I made for my little army would not work as long as we had the pups with us. We would simply have to go along with them and act according to the circumstances.

"Jamie," I started, "will you take a look through the windows and assess the situation, while the others and I go with Richard and Timothy? There is little more we can do with plans at this stage, for the pups will have no idea what we are up to. This is not too serious, for we are all aware of what is required of us, and must act as the situation demands."

"That's fine by me," said Jamie, and the rest of the pack chorused their agreement.

I heard a rustling and got to my paws, ready to do battle, but it was Pepi returning. He had two more golden Labradors at his heels. Their appearance was almost identical to that of Fred, and they carried just as much weight. I wondered if this was a Labrador trait, and came to the conclusion that it must be. Nevertheless, my small army had grown, and for that I was thankful.

"These two are Butch and Bruno," announced Pepi triumphantly.

"Pleased to meet you all," said the two Labradors politely.

We all introduced ourselves while the pups watched with interest, their conversation having dried up immediately upon Pepi's return.

"What can you tell us?" I asked the two newcomers, who were so alike I was having difficulty telling them apart.

"Well," began one of them, I think it was Butch, "you already know how many they are. They have taken our master and mistress captive and tied them up. The one who is injured, they have bandaged, but he is sleeping elsewhere in the house. The other three are talking about stealing the master's vehicle and taking the young pup across the border, wherever that might be. So we'll have to move fast."

While Butch spoke, I noticed a black spattering on his tongue and I realised that now it would be easy to identify him.

"I do not mean to be rude," I said, "but what is the matter with your tongue?"

"I was playing with the master," replied Butch with a chuckle. "He had dropped his plastic pen on the floor and when I picked it up, I crunched the outside of it in my excitement. It cut my tongue and the ink leaked into the abrasions, making a sort of tattoo."

We all laughed merrily while Richard and Timothy, oblivious to the source of our amusement, watched with amazed expressions upon their faces.

"That's so cool," said Timothy with a smile.

The sun was by now creeping down the sky to the west, hovering just above the treetops.

"How is your arthritis treating you?" I asked Buddy, for I could see the pain in her eyes.

"Oh, I'll be ok," she replied bravely.

Richard and Timothy got to their paws in a crouch.

"Come on you lot," said Richard, "enough of your games, we've got a job to do."

Every dog sprang to his or her paws instantly and followed the pups through the rest of the wheat in single file. When we arrived at the edge of the plantation, Richard stopped and Timothy moved up beside him. They peered through the remaining wheat stalks.

"If we head off to the left through the bushes, we can work our way around to the back of the barn," said Richard.

They took off in a running crouch toward the scrub, which bordered the large expanse of short-cropped green grass, marking the beginning of the garden. The pack of eleven now followed silently behind them. As we reached the bushes and took cover, Jamie branched off to the right, running low and darting from tree trunk to tree trunk, toward the farmhouse.

"Where's she off to now?" asked Richard.

"Must have their own plans, Rich," replied Timothy.

We crept quietly and apparently unnoticed through the bushes until we reached the side of the barn. Edging forward, Richard peeped around the corner. I was right beside him and could see the house off to the right. The only movement was Jamie making her way up to a window. I watched as she rose to her hind legs, her forepaws resting against the wall, and cautiously lifted her head above the window ledge, spying through the transparent material. She turned her head from side to side, sizing up the situation and then dropped to her four paws again, trotting to the right of the house and disappearing around the side.

There were two vehicles parked outside the house, between it and the barn. The one closest to the house was a large two-seater with ample room at the rear for storage of farm goods, while the second was more of a family vehicle.

"Wow!" said Richard, "an old Ford pick-up. That must be ancient."

"And that car's pretty old too," put in Timothy.

"Yeah, but that Ford looks vintage," said Richard, obviously knowing his vehicles.

"I wonder if it still runs?" asked Timothy.

"Well, if it does, it won't go very fast anymore," replied Richard.

"Since I know the area, let me lead the way," suggested Butch, coming up beside me.

He trotted off along the front of the barn, stopping a little way ahead, then vanishing into what must be a duoped door. The rest of us, led by Richard and Timothy, followed in single file once again.

Inside the barn were three horses, varying in size. The biggest one, and large he was indeed, had a glorious mane which hung down below his powerful neck. He was an impressive animal and his dark, almost black coat shone, for he was obviously well groomed and cared for. His long tail was as illustrious as his mane. The middle-sized one was a chestnut colour with a white star upon his forehead, white fetlocks, and black mane and tail, while the smallest pony, was again very dark. She had a sprinkling of white spots upon her rump, and looked rather aged.

"Hello Butch and Bruno," said the largest horse, "you've found a great many friends suddenly."

"'Afternoon Chimes," greeted Bruno, "they've all come to rescue a young duoped pup who is being held hostage in the farmhouse."

He continued his narrative, explaining the entire story, as far as he knew it, to the three horses who listened with polite interest.

"Just let us know if there's anything we can do to help," offered Chimes, a frown upon his magnificent forehead. His large dark eyes, framed by long lashes, revealed a soft and gentle temperament.

Richard and Timothy had crossed the barn and were standing petting the horses, running their paws down the long faces, and scratching behind the ears.

"They might come in handy, y'know Rich," suggested Timothy.

"I hope we don't have to use them, 'cause that'll mean we failed in our mission," said Richard.

"Let's put a bridle on a couple of them just in case," suggested Timothy.

"Ok," said Richard, moving over to the wall where the tack was hanging on some hooks.

Jamie unexpectedly rushed into the barn, panting heavily.

"They're getting ready to move out," she announced, "better get over there quickly, follow me."

Butch and Bruno hurried to the door ahead of her and, after checking that there was no duoped in sight, led the way over to the farmhouse. They skirted around the right side of the house, the way Jamie had gone, and to the front.

"We have the element of surprise, dogs," I said as we reached the door, which fortunately was open.

Suddenly we heard the roar of an engine.

"Oh no!" said Richard, "we're too late."

The pups hurried through the door, closely followed by the pack, all jostling to get through before the other. The little ones darting in beneath the bellies of the larger ones. It was chaotic. We dashed through one room and into the next, one where food is prepared. Sitting in two of the four chairs around a table, were a male and female duoped, whom I assumed must be Butch and Bruno's master and mistress, for their forepaws were tied behind their backs, and cloth covered their mouths. Through one door leading from the room we were in, I could see Potbelly slumped in a chair, apparently sleeping, and unaware of our presence. His wounds had been bound with cloth, but his face was pale. I concluded that the duopeds had decided it best to abandon him. There was no sign of Kim.

The sound of a vehicle speeding away could be heard, and I rushed to the back door just in time to see the old Ford disappear through the open gate in a cloud of dust. When I turned back into the room, Richard and Timothy were busy untying the duopeds.

"Where did you kids come from?" asked the male as Richard removed the cloth from his mouth.

"We've been following that rotten lot for days," replied Richard.

Timothy was busy helping the female.

"Thank you," she said, rubbing the area just above her forepaws when Timothy had finished.

The pups introduced themselves, extending their forepaws.

"My name is Owen and this is my wife Irene," offered the male duoped shaking paws with the pups.

"You all look tired and hungry," said Irene, "let me get you something to eat while Owen phones the police."

"Thank you," said Richard politely, "but I think we'd better get on after them or we'll lose them. Would you mind if we used two of your horses?"

"I don't think that would be such a good idea," replied Owen, "they don't get ridden much anymore, so they'll be unfit. They're not shod either, so they'll have trouble with the stony road. Anyway, it would be better to leave it up to the police," he continued as he walked over to the phone hanging on the wall.

Irene in the mean time was preparing sandwiches for the pups, having already placed a huge bundle of biscuits upon the floor for us, and we were munching away contentedly. Owen was jiggling the hand set up and down on the phone, apparently getting no response.

"I think they must have cut the line," he finally concluded.

"Then we have to get after them," said Timothy frantically, "please can we use your horses, we'll be very gentle with them."

"I think it best if you two stay here. I'll go after them in the old Pontiac. They won't get very far in the Ford; it's very low on fuel. The old gauge has stuck on full, but I know that it's nearly empty," said Owen.

"You have to take us with you, Owen," said Richard, sounding almost as frantic as Timothy.

I had been listening to the conversation when my attention was drawn to a sound I had not heard before in my long dog years. I sat peering out of the door, my head cocked to one side, trying to determine where the noise could be coming from. It was a drone, which was drawing closer and closer.

"Oh no," said Irene urgently, "the bees are swarming again."

"Quick!" said Owen, "close all the windows and doors, hurry!"

The two duopeds and the pups ran from room to room slamming doors and windows in a flurry, and completed their task none to soon. Before they had returned to the room where we were all waiting in confusion, swarms of tiny golden insects were pelting against the transparent material in the window frames. I had never seen the likes of it before. There were so many of them, but I could not understand the fear that I heard in the duopeds' voices.

"What is all the panic about, Butch," I asked.

"When the bees swarm like this they are deadly," offered Butch. "Each one of them only stings once, but as you can see there are so many that if one of us gets stung, the combined venom is enough to kill even a large duoped like my master. The likes of Pepi here, would probably only need five or six stings to extinguish his life," he continued gravely.

Richard and Timothy had returned and slumped down in two of the chairs around the table, looking totally deflated.

"How long will they keep this up?" asked Richard, a look of despair upon his young face.

"Sometimes they disperse after only a few minutes," offered Irene, "but quite often they hang around for much longer."

"Why don't you get rid of them?" asked Timothy.

"We've had bee-keepers come around so many times and seal up their hives, but they come back every year," said Owen.

"There's nothing to be done until they've gone," said Irene, "so why don't you just eat up your sandwiches and drink you milk. I'll give these dogs some more biscuits and milk too while you tell us all about your adventures."

Chapter Eight

I was becoming bored with listening to Richard and Timothy relating their tale, and so too, apparently, were the others. In fact, the only two quadrupeds who were paying any attention were Butch and Bruno. The rest of us, having had our hunger satisfied and our thirst quenched, were drowsing comfortably upon the clean tiled floor.

I was only half in a slumber when I become aware of a difference in the sounds outside. The persistent droning was diminishing and I could now hear the chirping of birds. I leapt to my four paws and cocked my head, looking up toward the window.

"They're leaving!" said Timothy excitedly, having noticed my renewed interest "please take us with you in the Pontiac."

"All right then," said Owen, getting up from the table and moving toward the door. As he opened it, there was a great rush of dogs pushing and shoving to get through first.

"They've thought of everything," said Owen, pointing to the old vehicle parked outside, "look, they've punctured all of the tyres."

"Oh, please let us take two of your horses," pleaded Richard, "we promise to be kind to them, but we can't just let those guys get away with Kim."

"Ok," said Owen resignedly, "You'd better take Gold Chimes and DJ, Petite is too old now. I'll help you saddle them up."

"Oh, we won't need saddles, we'll just ride bareback. Besides, it'll take too long and we've wasted enough time already," said Timothy eager to get moving.

"Well, I think it might be a good idea to have saddles, we can then attach saddle-bags to them and you can carry a few provisions with you," said Owen.

"Ok then," conceded Richard.

As the pups darted off toward the barn, I watched Owen wink at his wife and heard him whisper to her, "They'll never catch up with those villains so they'll be perfectly safe."

I wondered if they had any idea just how determined the two pups were.

My motley pack of dogs and I sat outside next to the old vehicle with its deflated tyres, and watched as the pups led the bigger horses out of the barn. Richard led the larger of the two, whom I had come to know as Chimes, while Timothy had the chestnut, whom I assumed must be DJ. The horses wore saddles and saddlebags upon their backs as I had seen done before, and had bridles over their heads with nasty looking metal bits inside their mouths, which I thought must be most uncomfortable. Owen gave them each a leg up in turn and the pups sat astride their steeds, ready to go forth into battle, resolute expressions upon their faces.

"Now you two boys go carefully, and remember that these horses can't have any water or large quantities of food just before they're about to be ridden. If you've found no trace of Kim by nightfall, come back here. I should have fixed these punctures by then," said Owen.

I looked up at the westerly sky, which was growing gloriously pink, and wondered what the purpose would be to head out now when there was so little left of the daylight, but said nothing.

"I've put some cubes into the saddlebags for the horses, though I don't think you'll need them," he continued.

"Wait a minute!" called Irene running from the back door of the farmhouse.

"I've put a few things together for the kids and the dogs. Pop them in the saddlebags for them," she said to Owen, handing over a number of packages, "and here's a flask of water too. I thought you might need these jackets, they used to belong to our boys when they were lads." She continued, handing two chunky jackets up to the pups.

Owen opened the saddlebags and placed the packages and flask inside, carefully strapping them up tightly again, while the pups tied the jackets around their waists with the sleeves.

"Thank you," said Richard and Timothy politely.

My army had collected closer together and awaited my instructions.

"Buddy, how is your arthritis, are you going to be able to keep

95

up with us? And what about you Jamie, are you recovered from your fall?" I asked, feeling concern for these two dear friends of mine.

"I'll be fine," said Buddy gallantly.

"I've completely forgotten my aches," replied Jamie.

"And you Labradors?" I asked, speaking to the four of them collectively, "I know not how fast we shall be travelling, nor how far. Would you prefer to remain here?"

"No!" they all replied in unison.

"We'll not let you down," said Fred.

"And what of you little ones? Your legs are much shorter, do you think you will cope?"

"I'm in," said Ruffles, enthusiastically.

"I won't be left out," added Snoopy.

"Nor I," said Pepi.

"You've got no chance leaving me behind!" said Oscar with his usual impudence.

Again I felt my heart bursting with pride for my brave furry friends.

"Then follow those horses, and do not spare the paws!" I said triumphantly, though I was unsure if I had quoted the duoped adage correctly.

Richard and Timothy gently nudged their steeds' ribs with their hind paws and moved forward, eleven dogs of different shapes and sizes following in a tight pack. The horses broke into a trot and I was surprised at how well the pups rode, posting along as one with the horse, looking perfectly comfortable. The speed was not too strenuous so the entire pack was following behind at an easy pace. As we passed through the farm gate, the pups turned in their saddles to wave their paws at Owen and Irene, who stood where we had left them, watching after us as we departed. They both raised their forelimbs and waved back at us.

"Have you got your McGuyver set with you, Tim? asked Richard.

"Yeah," replied Timothy, half turning to Richard, a broad grin on his face.

"Good stuff," said Richard, "that means we don't have to go back tonight."

I was somewhat confused and looked from one to the other of the canines, but none could enlighten me.

Immediately we were around a corner where the farmhouse could no longer be seen, the pups urged their horses on a little. Breaking into a gentle canter, the pups steered the horses to the side of the dirt road where the ground was less compacted, and thus gentler upon their steeds' hoofs. The speed was still not too uncomfortable for the dogs to keep up at this stage, and so the larger ones pushed on ahead of the horses, following the tracks that had been left by the old Ford. I was running along beside Gold Chimes, hoping to pick up on the pups' plans by eavesdropping on their conversation.

"Owen said they'd run out of fuel. I hope they don't manage to get too far," said Richard, "but if we don't catch up with them before dark, which isn't that long away, we'll set up a makeshift camp until dawn tomorrow."

The sky to the west was by now a deep purple as the sun had disappeared completely, and I knew it would soon be dark. We had not been travelling too long, but would shortly have to make camp, for travelling in the dark was not advisable; the horses could easily injure themselves. The pups had slowed their steeds to a trot, as the Labradors were lagging behind.

"What's that I can hear?" asked Timothy, pulling in DJ's reins and slowing to a halt.

Richard too, reigned in Chimes, and all the dogs stopped instinctively, heads cocked and listening intently.

"It's a gurgling sound," said Richard, dismounting from his horse.

Jamie was the first to leave the roadside, rushing through the dry bushes toward the sound.

"There's water coming out of the ground," she announced excitedly, standing over a small stream, the origin of which appeared to be directly beneath it.

The rest of the pack had arrived and were staring in amazement at the water gushing forth from the earth when Richard and Timothy came along on paw, leading Chimes and DJ.

"It's a spring!" said Richard eagerly, "that's great, we'll set up camp right here. The horses and dogs can have their fill of water."

"But don't forget that the horses can't have water just before we leave tomorrow", reminded Timothy.

I was mesmerised by the sight before my eyes. The water was crystal clear and bubbled briskly, releasing small tendrils of steam, which curled upward and then dissipated. The trees, shrubs and grass surrounding the spring were a luscious green, but many different shades and I looked forward to seeing it in the daylight when the colours would be even more vibrant.

While all the dogs were paddling around in the warm stream, chatting away happily to each other, Richard and Timothy unsaddled their horses, leaving the bridles on. The Labradors had all collapsed, bellies in the water, their tongues flopping out of their mouths, occasionally lapping up some of the clear, sparkling liquid. The pups led their steeds to a tall tree, tying their reins to a low branch, but leaving ample room for the horses to move around. They placed their saddles upside down on the ground, leaning them against the trunks of two other trees close by, laying the stuffed saddlebags beside them. A half moon was rapidly rising in the east, casting an eerie light over the land.

"Where's your McGuyver set?" asked Richard.

"Right here," replied Timothy, pulling out a small leather case from his trouser pocket.

"Let's find some dry pieces of wood and get a fire going," suggested Richard.

"But what if those guys see the flames, or even get a whiff of the smoke?" queried Timothy.

"I don't think we're that close to them yet, Tim. I don't even know if we'll ever catch up to them, but we're not going to give up, so we'll leave before the birds are up in the morning," replied Richard.

With that, the pups set off into the wilderness seeking dried fallen timber with which they could make a fire, and the pack of canines gathered around me for a conference, which was instinctive, rather than an instruction.

"I think we should send out a scout ahead of the pups tomorrow to see if there are any signs of the kidnappers," I suggested.

"I'll go," offered Jamie immediately, "I've got the longest legs."

"Good idea, Jamie, but I think I should be the one this time," I said.

"But then who will urge the slower ones on?" asked Ruffles.

"Well, you are always so full of energy, Ruffles, I think you would perform that task quite admirably," I replied, watching Ruffles' chest expand with pride at my compliment.

"Maybe it would be better if you and Jamie go together," said Snoopy, "I don't think it's a good idea for any of us to be out alone."

"Perhaps you are right," I agreed, "then it is settled. Immediately, when the pups begin their journey, Jamie and I will go on ahead."

There was a rustling sound coming from the direction that the pups had taken, and all dogs turned their heads, some on their four paws in readiness for any unexpected peril. Richard and Timothy emerged from the trees into the moonlight, wearing the jackets that Irene had given them, and carrying large bundles of logs, Timothy barely visible behind his burden. They dropped their logs and scouted around for some smaller twigs with which they would be able to light the fire more easily, and laid it all out, the smaller twigs first, and then the logs. Timothy again brought out the small leather case and opened the zipper revealing a number of tiny tools. However, it was the electronic lighter that he withdrew and handed to Richard.

"Thanks," said Richard, scraping some dried leaves together and pushing them beneath the small twigs. He flicked the lighter and held the flame to the kindling, which sputtered and smouldered at first, but finally a glow took hold, and smoke rose from the huge bundle. It was not much longer before flames licked up around the logs, crackling and sparkling, growing higher and stronger.

While Richard was seeing to the fire, Timothy went over to the horses, untied the reins and led them to the stream. Chimes and DJ drank thirstily, their muzzles buried deep into the water, sucking up the liquid with long slow intakes. Once they had had enough, Timothy took them back to the tree, where he once again tethered the reins loosely around the low branch.

"Right," said Timothy, "let's see what Irene has packed for us to eat."

He went across to the saddlebags and opened the buckles that secured them, pulling out the packages one by one. He picked up the one that contained the horse cubes and took them over to the horses, laying the food upon the ground before their forelegs. He undid the bridle buckle that secured the bit, allowing the horses freedom to eat. They munched their cubes contentedly.

"We'd better not eat too much tonight, we don't know how long we're going to be out on the road," said Richard, rising from his crouched position and moving over to where Timothy was sorting through the remaining packages.

"Yeah," agreed Timothy reluctantly, "but that goes for the dogs too."

All the dogs had assembled around the campfire expectantly, and groaned unhappily at this remark. Timothy had found the parcel of dog biscuits and began to share them out. He gave two each to Pepi and Oscar, an extra one each to Snoopy and Ruffles, and four each for the rest of us.

"Well, if that's dinner, I guess I've had it," grumbled Wilma who had bolted down her biscuits in record time, long before the rest of us had finished.

"Look at it this way," said Fred, who had also finished his scant meal, "we'll really look forward to breakfast tomorrow."

"The pups are right. We have no idea how long we will be out here, so we must ration our resources carefully." I said. "Now we had better settle down and get some sleep. We have an early start tomorrow, and possibly a long day ahead of us."

I watched as the pups chewed on some dried beef, my mouth watering, and my mind wandered to those good old days, which seemed so long ago, when food was plentiful and my basket with its ample blanket was awaiting me. I thought of Toby and Charlie back home and wondered if they were at all worried about us. I was sure they would be. I was looking forward to relating our tale to them and imagined Toby's aging aristocratic face, eyes gazing into mine in that customary feline manner, and Charlie, head cocked, straining to hear what was being said.

The night air had grown chilly, and we were grateful to have the fire around which we were all huddled. Richard and Timothy, their jackets drawn tightly closed across their chests, had settled down in front of the saddles, using them as backrests. Finally, satisfying myself that every dog and the pups were calm, I curled up and readied myself for sleep. I had only just gotten comfortable when Ruffles sneaked up and crept close, using my body to provide more warmth. I grumbled quietly, but offered no further resistance and we spent the remainder of the night snuggled closely together.

* * * * * * * * * * * * * * * * * * * *

Before the sun had risen, when the sky was not quite light, but the greyness was lifting gradually, I was awakened by the sound of a horse neighing. Startled by the unfamiliar noise, I leapt to my four paws, accidentally tossing Ruffles to the ground. He shook himself groggily and I marvelled at how deeply he slept.

"What's up?" he muttered.

"The pups are readying themselves to leave," I said, "better rouse the rest of these sleeping canines."

Ruffles shook himself once again, and then proceeded to nudge each of the dogs in turn. I decided to take the opportunity to sneak off into the bush so as to perform my morning ritual in relative privacy. I had only just completed my business when the rest of the pack began to disperse, presumably to conduct their private functions. The pups in the mean time were busy saddling the horses, and I wondered how and when those animals would have an opportunity to complete their bodily needs.

Timothy apportioned some biscuits in the same quantities as the previous night, and we all tucked in with great enthusiasm, devouring them in seconds. Richard moved toward the spring, the flask in his paws, obviously with the intention of filling it, and the canines took that as a lead, for they all headed that way themselves. As I had suspected, the spring with its surrounding foliage was a sight to behold, and the colours were indeed vibrant. Dew lay upon the grass, the birds in the trees just beginning to stir, and I fervently wished that I would one day have an opportunity to see this glorious place again in the full light of the day.

"Now remember, friends," I said, rousing myself from my reverie, "not too much liquid in your stomachs or you will no doubt end up with cramps."

I do not think any one of them paid heed to my warnings, for they drank with such gusto one would have thought they were camels. Richard and Timothy were washing their faces and drinking from the stream, having already replenished the flask.

Finally, the pups, their ablutions completed, and astride their steeds once again, the dog army clustered together in a safe pack, we left the clearing along the route we had come in on. When we came clear of the trees, which lined the dirt road, the pups steered their horses to the left and immediately broke into a gentle trot.

"I think we will let them stay ahead for a while," I suggested to Jamie, "then move on to the front of them."

"Fine by me," she replied.

The rest of the bunch settled into the same arrangement as the previous day, with the smaller dogs directly behind Jamie, Buddy and myself, while the Labradors brought up the rear.

The sun had not yet risen and the sky was still grey, though cloudless. The air was crisp and chill. I was watching the pups with growing respect. Their ability to control those horses was amazing. They sat bolt upright, their backs ramrod straight, rear limbs slightly bent and their knees tightly hugging the saddles. Their heels pressed down and level with the balls of their hind paws in the stirrups, turned inward slightly, all looked perfectly natural. They moved with the horses as one.

Then suddenly there was a rustling in the bushes to the right of the road and Chimes shied to the left, side stepping directly into DJ and knocking him off balance. The terror was visible in his eyes, with the whites showing. Richard was almost unseated, but his tight knees saved him and he clung on like a leech, but lost the reins and I could see him grappling to regain control. Eventually, he managed to get both paws on the reins and tugged hard, pulling Chimes' head sharply into his ample chest. But Gold Chimes is a powerful animal, broad across the shoulders with a thick neck, now arched and exhibiting those tremendous muscles. He was prancing around in sheer fright and then bolted off down the road at a full gallop, a great cloud of dust obscuring my view.

I worried that Richard might be unable to bring him under control, but my attention was immediately brought back to the scene around me. DJ had staggered from the blow and had not yet caught sight of the object of terror. As Chimes galloped off, however, DJ spied a movement in the bushes and, being already spooked, he reared up upon his hind legs, thrashing his fore legs in the air. Had Timothy not grasped a bunch of mane in his paw, he would surely have parted company with his steed. Timothy, too, had lost his grip on the reins, but had retained his pawing in the stirrups.

An animal darted out from the direction of the rustling and sped across the road in front of DJ, its furless tail standing straight up in the air, the tuft at its end waving from side to side. Timothy snatched up the reins and pushed himself forward upon DJ's neck, pulling down hard and forcing the horse to return to his four hoofs. DJ began backing up, totally oblivious of the dogs behind him. Buddy staggered out of the way, stepping back directly upon Oscar causing a ripple effect. Oscar tripped over Pepi and fell against Ruffles, who in turn tumbled against

Snoopy. Jamie, who thought she had escaped the skirmish, was now in line for Snoopy's lurching advance and as he fell against her legs, she lost her balance. The Labradors, who had been bringing up the rear as usual, were still in forward motion. Jamie staggered into Butch and the result was like dominos falling, until all the Labradors were upon each other in a heap of golden fur. Chaos reigned supreme as the strange creature, one I had never seen before, disappeared into the bush on the left side of the road. Timothy finally managed to take control once again, patting and stroking DJ along the neck; all the time talking in a soothing voice until the horse settled.

I was delighted when Richard returned to the group having succeeded in calming Chimes as well, and I was in awe at their expertise.

"It was a wart hog!" shouted Timothy excitedly and a little out of breath from his strenuous escapade.

"Wow!" said Richard, "we must be right out in the bush to see one of those."

"D'you think it was on its own?" asked Timothy.

"I shouldn't think so," replied Richard, "which way did it go?"

"In there," said Timothy, indicating the direction that the wart hog had taken.

"Let's go see if we can see it," suggested Richard, "it might have gone to join some others."

"Are you out of your minds?" I thought, "That creature had tusks!" Oh, how I wished I could communicate with these pups and advise them of the peril that lay ahead should they decide to take that path. Alas, my thoughts were unable to penetrate their minds and they steered their horses into the bush, following the wart hog's trail.

"We cannot allow those pups to go in there alone," I said to my soldiers. "But that creature could be extremely dangerous, so if any of you would prefer not to go, I shall fully understand."

"As you've told us before Digby, there's safety in numbers," responded Pepi.

"What guts you have," I said with genuine admiration for this tiny canine.

104

With that, we all followed along behind the horses, who were by now composed.

The pups gently reined in their steeds as we approached a clearing in the bush and all the dogs eased up beside them. The vision before us was astonishing. The hog that had startled the horses must have been a young one left behind, for there were seven or eight of the same size, with one much larger. They were all down on their knees, snouts muzzling the grass, and pulling out tufts by the roots. It was the most serene picture I had ever had the fortune to observe.

"It's a whole family," said Richard in a whisper, "see that big one? She's looking after all of her babies."

"Surely they can't all be hers?" asked Timothy.

"Yeah, each female has seven or eight babies at one time," replied Richard.

"They're so ugly!" said Timothy.

"Yeah," said Richard, "but quite cute too when you watch them. What they lack in looks, they make up for in personality."

The horses were standing quietly and the dogs moved up to peer through the scrub. The strange looking creatures seemed not to be perturbed by our presence, but continued grazing. Two of the young ones began a game, pushing and shoving each other. Their tusks apparently still too small to do any damage to each other, and they frolicked around, head butting and kicking their hind legs up into the air. A remarkable observation I made was that their tails only stood up straight when they ran; the rest of the time, they hung down, swishing from side to side, presumably to dispatch any flies lingering too long in that vicinity. I found the entire encounter the most interesting occurrence of my adventures to date. I know not how long we were all standing there watching the hogs, but it was some time before the pups tired of this wondrous experience of nature, and the sun had risen above the horizon before we turned and headed back toward the road.

"Wow, that was something, huh?" said Timothy as we reached the road.

"Yeah, I've never seen them up so close before," replied Richard.

"Maybe that's because we were on horseback," suggested Timothy.

"I thought the dogs might have worried them, but they didn't seem to bother about them either," said Richard.

"Funny how they go down on their knees," observed Timothy.

"Well, they wouldn't be able to eat the grass otherwise," said Richard.

"And those tails! I've never seen anything so funny!" said Timothy.

"Yeah," said Richard again, then "come on, we'd better get a move on, and keep a tight rein in case something like that happens again. The horses were really spooked by that."

The pups urged the horses on into a trot and I glanced over my shoulder at the pack of dogs behind me. They were all spurred into action immediately and I could almost feel the enthusiasm with which they ventured forth. I slowed my pace and allowed Ruffles to come up beside me.

"Jamie and I are going on ahead now, Ruffles. Keep an eye on those Labradors and make certain they do not lag behind." I said.

"Sure thing!" said Ruffles, eager to take charge of the pack in my absence.

I pushed on ahead, linking up with Jamie and Buddy at the head of the pack.

"Shall we?" I said to Jamie.

"You know I'd come with you," offered Buddy, "but I don't know how long my legs would last."

"Thank you Buddy, but you will do more good here setting the pace for the others," I responded, "and Ruffles may need a strong paw to assist with encouraging the Labradors."

With that Jamie and I nodded to each other, breaking into a gentle canter and easing past the horses.

"Where d'you think they're off to?" I heard Richard ask.

"On their own mission again," was Timothy's reply.

* * * * * * * * * * * * * * * * * * *

Our forward trek was uneventful, but long and arduous. The sun was by now half way up the sky and beating down upon us relentlessly. We had had to stop on two occasions to recover our breath and were desperately in need of a drink. The pads of our paws were becoming tender and raw despite the soft sands through which we travelled.

"It might still be winter, Digby, but being out in this sun for so long is killing me!" said Jamie.

"I understand fully," I agreed, "but we must persevere. We shall take another short break in the shade soon."

The tracks left by the old Ford were now obscured by hoof prints of many different animals, and I wondered if we would ever catch up with our target. Or if, in fact, Owen had been correct in assuming that the vehicle they had taken was low in fuel. Should he have been wrong, our efforts would all be in vain. I wished I could ask Toby his advice for I knew his feline wisdom would be accurate and his suggestions infallible. I suddenly realised how exhausted I must be. A dog thinking of a cat being superior indeed! With that thought in mind I was spurred on, unwilling to be beaten. It was only when Jamie, with laboured breath, spoke to me at my side that I became aware of how fast we were moving.

"Digby, we've got to stop!" she said, panting heavily.

"Sorry, Jamie," I said slowing down. "My mind had wandered."

"I wish I had the stamina you have, and at your age too!" she responded between gasps.

We stopped then, flanks heaving, tongues hanging from our mouths.

"Over there Jamie, lie down under the shade of that tree," I suggested, out of breath myself.

Jamie's limbs were quivering from the exertion as she walked unsteadily toward the tree I had indicated. Immediately she reached her destination she flopped down on her side, her four legs extended, her huge head resting upon the cool earth, breathing heavily. I moved in beside her and took on much the same pose, soon drifting off into a fitful sleep.

Chapter Nine

Digby! Wake up!" I heard, and slowly opened my heavy eyelids to see Ruffles standing over me.

"Are you OK?" he asked.

I tried to lick my lips but my tongue was dry and swollen, my head aching.

"Come on, Digby, get up!" said Ruffles.

I carefully lifted my pounding head and tried to focus my eyes. Standing behind Ruffles were the pups with the horses beside them, and the rest of the pack, all watching me with worried expressions upon their faces.

"This is a real life example of the hare and the tortoise," I thought to myself, but left the words unspoken.

I raised my shoulder from the ground and winced at the twinge that shot through the muscles there. My entire body was wracked with throbbing aches and pains. Gently, and rather shakily, I managed to rise to my four paws, my limbs quivering, not knowing where I was for the moment. Then I suddenly remembered Jamie and turned, a little too quickly I fear, to see if she was all right. My hasty movement toppled me off balance and I staggered, falling to a sitting position.

Richard handed his reins to Timothy and went to the saddlebags to retrieve the flask of water. He moved slowly toward me, opening the lid of the flask. Crouching in front of me he gently took my snout and pried open my jaws with the talons of his paws, carefully pouring some water into my mouth. It tasted exquisite, and I drank thirstily. As he withdrew I licked my lips, and although my tongue was still swollen, it was at least wet.

Richard then moved across to Jamie, who was still asleep, lying prone on the ground. He ran his paw across her shoulder, talking to her quietly. When she finally stirred, he helped her lift her huge head from the earth and repeated his actions, allowing water to slop into her mouth. Jamie too licked her lips and wagged her long tail, thumping it upon the ground in gratitude.

"Are they going to be alright?" asked Timothy, concern audible in his voice.

"Yeah, they'll be fine, but we have to find some more water soon," replied Richard.

I looked up at the sky to establish the position of the sun and was astounded to see that it had moved beyond the half way mark and was almost directly above us. I rose again to my four paws and encouraged Jamie to do the same.

"I am so sorry Jamie, through my intense desire to catch those villains, I have succeeded only in exhausting us and achieved nothing," I said.

"I'll be fine Digby," she responded kindly.

Richard, having stood up on his hind legs when Jamie rose, now bent over once again and gave her a little more water, then moved across to me to perform the same kind deed.

"Come on then Rich," said Timothy, "let's get a move on."

"OK," said Richard, "I think we've walked these horses enough now, let's mount up again and head out."

The pups placed their left hind paws into the stirrups and swung their right over the saddles, simultaneously heaving themselves upward. They took up the reins and steered the horses back onto the road, but continued at a walk, apparently considering the condition of Jamie and I. I was feeling quite ashamed of myself, being the leader of the pack, and having messed up so badly. Even the Labradors had done well in keeping up with the horses, though they were looking a little worse for wear by now.

"Did you find anything of interest?" asked Snoopy.

"Nothing," I replied despondently, my head hanging low in humiliation.

"Well, we had some fun and games," offered Pepi cheerfully.

"Oh," I said, "What happened?"

"A rabbit rushed out onto the road startling the horses again," began Buddy moving up beside me. "The pups were ready for it this time so they kept control well, but the little ones, Oscar and Pepi, instinctively took chase. Ruffles and Snoopy contained themselves for only the briefest of moments before they too scampered off into the bush after it."

"Ruffles had been doing such a good job keeping the Labradors moving, that when he disappeared, these lazy lumps took it as an opportunity to relax," said Snoopy, with affection in his voice.

There were some embarrassed chuckles from behind me and I turned to see the four Labradors cringing beneath their fur coats.

"Ahem…" began Fred, looking a little sheepish, "we thought we would just wait for them to come back."

"Only you never communicated your intentions to the pups," I suggested, beginning to get the gist of the situation.

"Exactly," said Fred. "So when they moved out with Buddy at their hoofs, we found a shady spot and took a nap."

"Of course, by the time we'd given up the chase, we were well ahead of the horses and found we had to wait for them along the road," said Ruffles.

"We noticed immediately that the Labradors were missing," put in Oscar.

"So we had to try and stop the horses, so we could go back and fetch these four," continued Ruffles.

"Pepi ran alongside Chimes and explained the situation to him, so he stopped," said Snoopy, "but Richard didn't know what was happening, so he kept urging Chimes on, and they were all going around in circles. It was the funniest thing I have seen in a long time."

"Then, Timothy realised that we were missing some dogs, and finally understood what was happening," put in Ruffles.

"So he told Ruffles to go find them," said Pepi, "while they moved over into the shade of a tree to wait."

"Buddy and I headed off down the road again, and eventually found four Labradors, snoring their heads off," said Ruffles.

"Rousing them from their sleep was bad enough," said Buddy, "but getting them on their four paws again was another story. I had to use my nose to physically push them off their bottoms, and then use some very stern words to get them moving."

I turned back again to peer at the Labradors, and they all grinned at me.

"You are a wonderful bunch!" I said, suddenly realising what they were up to, "you are all telling me this so that I will feel better."

"Well, do you?" asked Wilma with that beguiling smile of hers.

"Very definitely, thank you all." I said, feeling almost dog again.

As we rounded the next corner, the pups began shouting with glee, and Chimes and DJ broke into a gallop. I could barely see through the dust they kicked up behind them, but was able to make out the shape of a vehicle in the distance.

"Are you up to this Jamie," I asked, excitement welling up inside me.

"Right there beside you boss!" she replied.

Even the Labradors were running, albeit in a sort of side step.

It was indeed the old Ford, and as there was no visible damage to it, we assumed that it had run out of fuel. The pups had reined in the horses and dismounted in one movement.

"Y'know we should've come in more carefully," said Richard a little belatedly, "those guys could be in the bush watching us."

"I don't think so, Rich, they must've arrived here yesterday evening. They'll have moved on this morning," replied Timothy.

"Let's see if they've left anything we can use," suggested Richard.

"What's that big drum in the back?" asked Timothy.

Richard clambered up onto the back of the pick-up and examined the drum. He banged the side of it with his paw to ascertain if there was anything inside. The reverberation indicated that there was indeed some form of liquid within its confines.

"Well, it can't be fuel," said Richard, unscrewing the cap on the top of the drum, "or they'd be real dummies!"

He bent forward over the hole and sniffed.

"There's no smell at all," he said, "I think its water!"

Timothy dropped DJ's reins and was up on the back of the pick-up as quickly as a monkey would have been.

"Grab the flask Tim and help me empty some of this stuff into it," said Richard.

Timothy dashed back to the side of the vehicle and called to Chimes, who had wandered off to the edge of the road with DJ and was grazing peacefully on the tufts of grass. He immediately walked over to the Ford and Timothy unbuckled the saddlebag retrieving the flask and patting Chimes heartily along the neck.

The drum was obviously quite heavy for it took the two of them to tip it up enough to have the liquid flowing from the hole in the top.

"That's not going to be enough y'know Rich," said Timothy, "we've got all these dogs to think about."

"We'll just have to pour some down their throats before we head off again," replied Richard.

Timothy stood thinking about it for some time, a frown furrowing his young forehead. Then, suddenly, he leapt off the back of the pick-up and stared down at the wheels. Without wasting any time, he pulled his McGuyver set out of his pocket, unzipped it and withdrew a small spanner.

"What're you up to?" asked Richard.

"If we can get these hub-caps off, we can use them as dishes for the dogs to drink from," replied Timothy.

Richard landed upon his hind paws beside Timothy in a flash and watched as he pushed the spanner between the wheel and the hub, trying to pry them apart. Timothy was having great difficulty, as the spanner was not long enough and provided little leverage. Richard looked around and then jumped to his paws and rushed over to a large stone lying on the road. He picked it up and returned to Timothy's side.

"Use this to bang the spanner," he suggested.

"Good idea!" said Timothy, taking the stone from him.

He first used the stone to bang the spanner further in between the wheel and the hub then used it to bang the side of the spanner. The small tool began to bend.

"Hang on," said Richard, "there must be tools in the Ford somewhere."

He moved to the front of the vehicle and opened the driver's side door, pulled the backrest forward and reached in behind it.

"Bingo!" he shouted, as he pulled a large black plastic container out from where he had been looking. He untied the two laces, which bound it, and crouched on the ground where he emptied the contents of the bag.

"Here you are," he said, choosing a crowbar from the assortment of tools before him.

Timothy got to his hind paws and went across to Richard, who was still crouched over the implements.

"That'll do it," he said, taking the crowbar from Richard.

He returned to the rear wheel where his bent spanner was still lodged, and pried the larger tool in beside it. The hub sprang off the wheel, bouncing and then spinning away, finally coming to rest with a great clatter. He then moved to the front wheel where, after performing the identical task, he exacted the same result.

"Two should be enough, shouldn't it?" he asked.

"Yeah, they'll just have to take it in turns," said Richard, still examining the tools.

My soldiers were all clustered together, eagerly awaiting the much-needed water, and watched, tongues hanging out, as Timothy again leapt up into the back of the pick-up.

"I'll need a hand with this Rich," said Timothy, placing the two hubs on the floor in front of the drum.

"Coming," said Richard. He was holding a large wheel spanner, turning it over and over in his paw, staring off into space apparently deep in thought.

"What're you doing?" asked Timothy, glancing over the side at Richard.

"There're are a few things in here that may come in handy," he replied as he stood up, "I think we should take them along with us."

He climbed into the back of the Ford beside Timothy and between the two of them they decanted some water into the two hubs. The sound of water sloshing from the drum was like music to my ears.

Timothy hopped over the edge, landing nimbly upon his hind paws on the ground. Richard carefully handed the two hubs containing the water to Timothy, who just as cautiously, placed them on the ground, not spilling a drop. The canines watched every move, but remained in their positions, politely awaiting an invitation to partake of the life preserving liquid.

"We should do this in an orderly fashion," I suggested. "Two at a time, beginning perhaps in an alphabetical arrangement. That way there can be no favouritism. Bruno and Buddy can take the first turn."

Without further ado, the two elected dogs moved forward and drank thirstily from the makeshift bowls. Immediately, when they had finished, they moved back to their original places within the pack. Timothy picked up the hubs and handed them to Richard, then jumped back into the Ford to assist with the decanting once again. They duplicated the procedure of placing the hubs upon the ground, again not spilling a drop. Butch and I were next in line and I have to confess that the water tasted exquisite.

"Look at this Rich," said Timothy, "they're taking it in turns, two at a time."

Richard moved to the edge of the pick-up and peered over.

"Wow! You'd think they actually know what they're doing," he responded.

All the dogs chuckled, Fred giving a hearty chortle.

The process was repeated until finally Wilma had her turn.

"I'm so thirsty, I could drink that whole drum of water," she said as she waddled across to the hub.

"Do you think they've had enough?" asked Timothy.

"Let's fill two more and see if there're any takers," suggested Richard.

Every dog wanted some more and took their turns in the same order as before.

"What about the horses?" Timothy asked.

"They normally only drink once or twice a day, but they've been very active today so they might want some," said Richard, "but then again, I'm not sure if they should have any if we're going to ride them afterwards."

"Let's see if they want, if they do, we'll just walk them for a while," suggested Timothy.

"That's cool," said Richard.

As it turned out, Chimes and DJ were more interested in munching on the brown grass at the edge of the road, so the pups drank their fill of water from the flask and topped it up again from the drum. After carefully placing it in the saddlebag, Richard moved over to the tools, which still lay scattered across the ground. He picked up the crowbar, large spanner and a small axe and packed them away in the saddlebag. Timothy in the mean time was inside the cab of the Ford feeling under the seat for anything that might be useful. Finally he opened the glove box.

"Look! They must have forgotten this," said Timothy gleefully holding up a parcel wrapped in brown paper.

"What's that?" asked Richard.

"Biltong!" said Timothy.

Just the thought of dried meat got the taste buds working overtime and my mouth watered endlessly. As I glanced around at the other canines, I saw that they were all having the same reaction, the Labradors licking their chops hungrily.

"Anything else in there?" asked Richard.

"A packet of dried sandwiches," replied Timothy.

"I'm sure the dogs will enjoy those," suggested Richard.

"Ok," said Timothy as he retrieved the package from the vehicle and began sharing out the contents according to the size of each dog. The bread was a little dry, but when you are as hungry as we all were, food was food and no dog was fussy.

"We'd better get a move on," said Richard.

"How far do you think they are ahead of us?" asked Timothy.

"Well, they've got Kim to carry. She was weak when we last saw her, so there's no chance she'll be able to walk on her own. Apart from Kim, they're obviously travelling light, but they don't have the advantage of horses like we have, so we're definitely catching up with them. We'd better be careful. Maybe by nightfall we'll know where they are. Keep your eyes peeled for any signs of them from now on," said Richard.

The pups walked across to Chimes and DJ and swung up into the saddles. Back on the road again, trotting comfortably behind the horses, I glanced up at the heavens to ascertain the time. The sun was halfway down the western sky, but to the south I noticed some ominous cloud build-up. This could well mean a very cold night ahead of us.

* * * * * * * * * * * * * * * * * * *

We had stopped twice for a breather along the way, but the remainder of our journey had been uneventful that day. The sun had by now dropped down to the horizon and a deep pink haze hung in the sky to the west. The clouds that I had watched approaching from the south were heavy and dark. They had been moving rapidly across the heavens and threatened bad weather. Indeed, the evening air had taken on quite a chill already.

"I see a bad moon a rising, I see we're in for nasty weather," sang Fred cheerfully.

"I see a bad moon a rising, I think there's trouble on the way," continued Wilma in a singsong voice.

"What are you two on about?" I asked.

"There's a bad moon on the rise, the end is coming soon!" concluded Fred.

The two Labradors looked quite comical, putting a little waggle on as they sang.

"All right, what is this all about?" I asked again, unable to keep a smile from slipping onto my face.

"It's a song we often hear the duopeds singing," replied Wilma, smiling back at me.

"Those dark, heavy clouds reminded me of the words, though I doubt we got them correct," went on Fred.

"We've been watching you glancing up at the sky every now and then. You're obviously concerned about the weather so we thought we'd put a lighter note into the day," offered Wilma.

"The words of that song hardly put a lighter note on things," I said, enjoying their banter.

The rest of the pack laughed at this comment and Ruffles wagged his Basil Brush tail, which was beginning to look decidedly raggedy by now, in appreciation. The pups turned in their saddles, glancing over their shoulders, to see what all the noise was about.

"They seem to be having fun," observed Richard.

"Yeah, a strange bunch of dogs," said Timothy, "d'you think we should look for a spot to camp out for the night?"

"I suppose we should. It looks like we're in for nasty weather," said Richard.

The entire pack of dogs stopped in their tracks, looked at one another, and roared with laughter. Wilma had an attack of the giggles, which became contagious, until every one of us was helpless with mirth. This time the pups reined in their horses and turned fully around, expressions of amazement upon their young faces. Oscar was lying upon the dirt, his legs jerking spasmodically as he laughed with a total lack of control, while Butch sat on his haunches, his chubby tummy bouncing up and down in rhythm to his hoots of enjoyment. It was many minutes before we were able to take charge of ourselves, and all the time Richard and Timothy watched, their mouths curled up at the corners in smiles that I had never seen them use before.

Those few magical moments passed with the sound of a low rumble from the heavens above, and the final chuckles died away. We all looked at the pups expectantly, wondering what the next move would be.

"Ok," said Richard, "better find somewhere for shelter."

"There're some huge rocks over there that might be ok," said Timothy pointing to a rocky outcrop some distance off the road.

"Well, let's go and have a look then," suggested Richard.

They turned the horses and headed in that direction, all the dogs following in single file. The bush was much thicker here than we had seen during our travels, with low scrub and only a few tall trees. The ground had become quite sandy too, easier under paw.

"This looks like the best we're going to find," said Richard as he reined in Chimes, a few paces from an enormous boulder.

"There's a bit of an overhang there," said Timothy, "it might at least keep us dry."

"We're not likely to get any rain at this time of the year, Tim, but I suppose it might drizzle a bit," said Richard as he dismounted from his horse.

"Whatever, but it'll be jolly chilly tonight," responded Timothy.

"Yeah, better collect some wood for a fire," said Richard.

Timothy dismounted then and led the two horses to a tree where he tethered them and began unsaddling them. Richard came across and took off the saddlebags, carrying them to the overhang. Ducking beneath the rock he scrambled inside and began rummaging through the contents.

Snoopy was standing just beyond the great rock, his nose in the air, sniffing. I watched with interest for he too had taken on the stance of a pointer, a bird hunting dog, in the same fashion as Ruffles had earlier.

"Is there something wrong Snoopy?" I asked.

"Not sure," he replied, "there's something in the air, but I can't place it yet."

Standing beside him now, I too raised my nose to the air and sniffed. There was indeed an odd scent, but I could not ascertain what it might be.

"Come on dogs!" called Richard, "I've got some biscuits for you."

Snoopy and I turned in time to see the Labradors dashing in that now familiar gait toward Richard, followed by Jamie, Buddy, Pepi, Oscar and Ruffles. Richard had already shared out some biscuits, allowing an extra one for each dog.

"Since you've all been so good today, there's a treat for you," he said, placing some food in front of each dog.

Timothy walked across carrying a saddle.

"These need to be kept dry so I'll put them under the rock. We can use them as back rests again," he suggested.

"Here," said Richard, "take some cubes for the horses."

Timothy put some cubes into his jacket and carried it over to the horses where he poured them upon the earth for the horses to munch on. He then returned with the second saddle and placed it beside the first.

"We'd better clear away some of this scrub to make a clearing for a fire. We don't want to set the whole place alight," said Richard.

"That was the smell!" said Snoopy eagerly. "The one we couldn't recognise. It's the smell of cut or broken grass and branches."

"Oh no," said Ruffles, swallowing the last of his biscuits. "What does that mean?"

"That there are either some very large animals or duopeds in the vicinity, breaking down trees and bushes," I offered.

118

"We'll have to stop the pups from making any noise," suggested Fred, "but how're we going to get the message across?"

Richard appeared from the rock overhang with the axe in his paw, closely followed by Timothy who was carrying the crowbar. Butch and Bruno, who had been listening closely to our conversation, lunged forward, knocking the tools from the pups paws. Both pups took a step back looking in shock at the Labradors.

"What's this?" asked Richard, a glimmer of alarm in his eyes for he knew not these two canines or their habits.

"I don't think they want to hurt us Rich," suggested Timothy.

"Then what're they doing?" asked Richard.

"Not sure, let's try again," said Timothy.

Buddy and Snoopy moved up beside the Labradors and as the pups bent down to retrieve their tools, the four of them snarled viciously. The pups snatched back their paws in an instant.

"What's going on?" it was Timothy this time.

"Digby and Ruffles are just standing there watching all this," said Richard. "Surely they wouldn't let them hurt us."

Ruffles and I immediately moved forward and stood beside the four dogs guarding the tools. Richard gingerly reached forward to pet my head and I licked his paw affectionately. He then leaned to one side, still petting my head, and tried to uplift the axe with his other paw. I growled, baring my teeth and he withdrew carefully.

"What do you think of that?" he asked of Timothy.

"He seems to agree with the others. They don't want us to do anything with those tools for some reason," Timothy replied.

Pepi suddenly rushed out of the undergrowth, stumbling over some low branches, and landing in a heap at my forepaws. I had not even noticed his departure.

"They're really close!" he gasped, regaining his paws. "Not far from here. They're setting up a camp of their own!"

"I wish I knew what was going on," said Richard watching these events unfolding before his eyes.

"You must take me there, Pepi," I said. "Ruffles, come with us, but the rest of you must stay here and look after the pups. Do not allow them to move, even if you have to sit upon them to keep them here. We shall return soon."

The three of us darted off into the bush, Pepi in the lead.

"They're not far so keep quiet," said Pepi in a whisper.

"Is it still just the three of them with Kim?" I asked quietly.

"I didn't waste any time checking that out. I wanted to come back and tell you straight away," he said.

"A very wise decision," I congratulated him.

Pepi had slowed down and was stepping gingerly through the undergrowth, making virtually no sounds, so Ruffles and I followed suit. After a short distance he stopped and turned his head in our direction.

"They're just the other side of that bush. If we go around the right side of it, we can watch them from the cover of some undergrowth," he whispered, his voice barely audible.

He crept cautiously forward and around the side of the bush, Ruffles and I at his heels equally silent. Once we were in position I could see between the low twigs. Fur-face was crouching over a mound of blanket upon the ground, which I assumed must be Kim. Baldy was busy arranging some branches for a fire in the open space that they had created. Goliath was collecting dead leaves for kindling from the other side of the clearing.

"I'm worried about this child, she hasn't eaten anything in days," said Fur-face.

"Pour some water down her throat and she'll be fine," suggested Goliath.

"We have to keep her alive or she's no good to us," said Baldy, "so make sure you get something down her gullet."

Fur-face rose to his hind paws and moved away from Kim, revealing some provisions and a water canister, larger than the flask that the pups had, but not too large for a dog to carry.

"We need Jamie here," I whispered, "Ruffles will you go and fetch her?"

"Sure thing!" he replied eagerly and turned to leave.

Pepi and I watched as Baldy struck a match and held it to the kindling, almost burning the talons of his paw before a flicker took hold, and then a flame licked up around the logs.

It was only a few minutes later that Ruffles returned with Jamie in tow.

"Is everything all right back there? Are those canines keeping control of the pups?" I asked.

"I think they know why we're holding them there now. They talked of the smell of
smoke, so they have realised that there are other duopeds in the area," said Ruffles.

"What did you want me for? I am here at your command master!" said Jamie playfully.

"Do you see those provisions over there beside that mound of blanket?" I asked.

"Sure do," she replied.

"Be very careful, for I think that is in fact Kim beneath that blanket. We are in dire need of some water and food if we are to succeed in our quest. As the best thief on the block, I am hoping you will be able to steal as much as possible without being seen," I said.

"Well, that is a backhanded compliment if ever I heard one," said Jamie, "but I am that hungry that I'll do it with pleasure. Now watch the expert in action!"

She carefully manoeuvred her great paws through the undergrowth, and as quiet as any thief, disappeared around the side of the clearing. We watched from our hiding place as the duopeds huddled around the now roaring fire, warming their paws. Shortly after her departure, we saw a glimpse of Jamie on the other side, stealthily edging forward toward the provisions. None of the duopeds noticed her approach. She was crawling on her tummy, like a lion stalking its prey. The silence was deafening. Delicately, Jamie placed her huge jaws around the water canister and edged her way back into the undergrowth. We waited impatiently for the next move. I spied her peering through the branches, making certain that she would not be spotted. Then she emerged once more, using the same method. She carefully uplifted a package and retreated again into concealment. I was more than impressed.

"She will be unable to carry all that on her own," I said to Pepi and Ruffles, "so I shall go and give her a paw."

I moved as quickly, but as quietly as possible. When I arrived at Jamie's hiding place, she was busy stealing yet another package. I waited impatiently for her return.

"We cannot carry any more than that," I said, "let us get back to the others before the duopeds discover their rations missing."

As my jaws were not large enough to get around the water canister, Jamie picked it up in hers and I carried the two packages together, using the ends of the packets for holding devices. We silently moved through the bushes, all the time aware of the duopeds to our right. When we arrived at the spot where Pepi and Ruffles were awaiting our return, I dropped the two packages and asked Ruffles to take charge of one. Without further ado we headed back to the rock overhang where the rest of the hunting party were holed up.

The pups were sitting beneath the overhang talking quietly and the dogs were lying upon the ground totally relaxed when we returned. The evening was darkening rapidly now and the chill air was becoming icy. I guessed that as the sky was so heavy with clouds, the moon would have little effect and I was grateful that canines had better vision in the dark than did duopeds.

"The pups seem to have accepted their fate," said Fred, lazily. Then noticing the provisions we carried, he leapt to his paws in an instant. "Have you found food?" he asked excitedly.

The other three Labradors were at Fred's side immediately, with Wilma at the fore, her doe-like eyes large with expectation. The chuckle that gurgled up into my throat nearly choked me and I was forced to drop my parcel. Regaining my self-control, I picked it up again and followed Jamie and Ruffles to the pups. The three of us placed our burdens upon the ground in front of the pups' hind paws.

"They must have found those villains!" said Timothy.

"Yeah, but how did they get this stuff away without being seen?" Richard asked.

"Well, I guess we'll never know that," said Timothy, "but maybe the dogs will show us where they are."

Both pups reached out and patted the dogs closest to them.

"Well done!" they said together.

"Let's see what they've found," suggested Richard.

Richard opened the first package and found three cold pork sausages, four hard-boiled eggs, two bananas and an apple.

"They must have raided Irene's fridge before they left," he said.

The package that Timothy opened contained an assortment of sandwiches, but the corners of the bread were all curled up.

"They must have had Irene make them some sandwiches too," he remarked, "some of them are half eaten."

"This water canister is almost full," said Richard. "That's great, we'll have enough to feed and water the dogs and us before we go into battle."

They both laughed at this last remark.

"Don't forget we still have quite a lot of that biltong as well," reminded Timothy.

"Yeah, but we'll leave that till last, 'cause it'll make us real thirsty," put in Richard.

The entire pack of dogs had gathered around the pups, saliva drooling from the Labradors' lower jaws. Timothy shared out the sandwiches proportionately according to the size of each dog and fed us all individually, while Richard shared out the food from his package.

"Give me your McGuyver knife, Tim, and I'll cut the apple and one sausage in half," said Richard.

Once we had finished gorging ourselves, Richard unscrewed the cup from the top of the water canister and poured some water into it. He handed it to Timothy who drank first, then had some himself. He then poured some more into the container and allowed each dog in turn to have as much as they required. The pups ate their ration of food and then lay back against the saddles for a few minutes. The canines all got comfortable; some of them drifting off to sleep and snoring lightly in contentment.

"We'll have to go in search of their camp, Tim," suggested Richard after a little while, his eyes closed.

I immediately rose to my four paws and moved over to his side, nudging him with my snout. He reached out and stroked the fur along my neck.

"What's the matter Digby?" he asked, without moving another muscle.

"I wish we knew the rest of their names," said Timothy, "they're all so friendly."

I snuggled in closer and rested my head lightly upon Richard's shoulder, enjoying the petting.

I must have drifted off to sleep, for I was awakened by Pepi, who was whimpering at my side.

"What is the matter?" I asked, carefully lifting my head, not wanting to disturb Richard from his slumber.

"I have been spying on those villains," he reported, a little out of breath.

"And what have you established?" I asked, sitting up immediately.

"They have discovered the provisions missing," he began, "but at this stage they think it must have been a hyena because of the paw print size. But they're very suspicious and talking about us. They reckon that they would have smelt a hyena."

"Then it is time to make our move. Well done, Pepi!" I said. "Gather these sleeping beauties together as quietly as possible while I rouse the pups."

Pepi moved from one sleeping dog to the other, waking each with a gentle nudge. I was amazed at how silent each was as they amassed in a group awaiting further instructions. I gently nudged the pups, who rose to a sitting position, rubbing their eyes.

"What's up?" asked Timothy, noticing all the canines gathered together.

"Don't know," said Richard, "but we've trusted these mutts all the way here, so I guess we should do so now."

I turned to address my soldiers.

"I think we must surround their camp since they have become suspicious about our presence. We have the element of surprise; they will not be expecting an attack during the night, especially one as dark as this. In addition, we will be able to see from the light of their fire, while they will be looking directly into blackness. Absolute quiet is of the essence, dogs. Ruffles and I will lead the pups for they know us, the rest of you must act according to instinct.

I know you will all do the right thing," I concluded.

Without a sound, the dogs disappeared into the night, breaking off, each taking different routes. I glanced at the pups then crept quietly in the direction of the camp, Ruffles at my flank. The pups followed in an upright stance, but were quiet. As we drew closer to our target, I crouched in a catlike pose and crawled a few feet forward. Looking over my shoulder, I noticed that Ruffles had assumed the same posture, and the pups had gone down on their forepaws and knees.

Although we could hear voices, we were unable to distinguish the words being spoken, but as we reached the spot where we had spied upon the duopeds previously, the words became clearer.

"I'm telling you, we would have smelt it if it was a hyena, those things stink!" came Goliath's now familiar voice.

"I agree," put in Fur-Face, "with all that rotten meat they eat, it clings to their fur."

"Well, I don't see how those kids and dogs could have caught up with us," said Baldy, "besides, those paw marks we found were too big for a dog."

"Now we've got nothing to eat or drink, and nothing to give the girl," said Fur-face rather forlornly.

"We can't be that far from civilization," said Baldy, "we'll leave early in the morning and find another farmhouse somewhere. We might even be lucky and cadge another vehicle."

And so the conversation droned on.

"What're we going to do?" asked Timothy in a whisper.

"They don't have their guns on them. Look they've left them lying over there beside Kim," said Richard. "It looks as if the dogs have surrounded the camp so maybe we could charge from all angles, it should cause enough confusion for us to snatch Kim."

"But how will we get her away?" Timothy queried.

"We've got the horses, remember. We can use one of them to carry her back to Irene and Owen," said Richard.

"You don't think those three will just lie back and let us take her away do you?" asked Timothy.

"Of course not!" Richard replied. "The dogs can guard them with one of us while the other takes Kim away."

125

"That might work, if we can get hold of the guns," said Timothy.

I was listening to the pups' conversation, my brain running around inside my head trying to find a solution to the problem, when an idea suddenly came to mind.

"Ruffles go and find Fred." I said, "tell him that he and either Butch or Bruno, one of them must have the same talents as he, must make a dash for it and snatch up the guns."

The pups were still discussing their options as Ruffles crept silently away, when mayhem descended upon the scene.

One of the dogs must have disturbed a rabbit, for it darted into the campsite, startling the duopeds. The three of them shot up, Goliath and Baldy diving for the guns, Fur-face in some apparent confusion, turning around in circles. The two with the guns stood back to back, forelimbs outstretched, grasping the weapons, which were aimed at the perimeter of the campsite. Not a dog, or a pup moved. The only sound to be heard was the crackle of the fire.

Then suddenly, I heard a movement to my right, the stamping of hoofs. A large animal it must have been, for the sound was deafening in the quiet. My heart thumped in my chest and my mouth went dry. The two armed duopeds swung around, both pointing their guns in the direction of the noise. The sound of snorting came from the bushes and I cringed against the pups' sides. I could feel their nervousness.

Gold Chimes erupted from the bushes into the clearing with DJ at his flank. The duopeds scattered and the dogs were spurred into action. Jamie flew through the air at tremendous speed, colliding with Baldy and knocking him clean to the ground, the gun spinning out of his paw and crashing into a shrub, lost in the dark. At the same moment Fred, Buddy and Butch launched an attack on Goliath, who was still armed. He turned, aiming the gun at the three dogs approaching him, and I grasped the moment. My fear forgotten, I galloped through an opening and threw myself at his extended forelimb, sinking my teeth in as I connected. The weapon dropped to the ground at the same moment that the three heavy dogs crashed into the huge duoped. Goliath went down with a thunderous, nerve-shattering crunch, and I heard the air leaving his lungs in a great whoosh.

Jamie, who was still grappling with Baldy, was joined by Bruno and Snoopy, and between the three of them, were able to contain him. The pups were wrestling with Fur-face, Pepi, Oscar and Ruffles attacking his hind paws and legs. He managed to fling the pups off temporarily, but kept stumbling with the little canines hanging on to his trouser legs. As he scrambled toward the edge of the clearing, Chimes moved with immense decorum across his path, preventing any further advance. The expression of panic upon the duoped's face was a picture, as Chimes glared at him with contempt. After terrorising Fur-face for a few more seconds, Chimes gave him a good nudge, sending him flying back into the centre of the clearing where the pups pounced upon him once again. The little canines returned to their favourite position and assisted in the confinement of the duoped by restricting the movement of his legs.

As the dust began to settle, I glanced around the campsite. It was a sight to behold. The fire crackled merrily, oblivious to any of the goings-on around it. The rabbit had disappeared as quickly as it had appeared. Goliath lay flat on his back gasping for breath, which was not surprising since he had Fred and Wilma stretched across his belly, and Butch and Buddy lay across his legs. Baldy was also prone upon his back with Jamie's great jaws around his throat, Bruno across his stomach and Snoopy holding down his legs. The pups had Fur-face in a sitting position, his arms pinned back behind him, and his legs secured by three little dogs enjoying ripping his trouser legs to shreds. The two horses stood at attention at the edge of the clearing, guarding the scene and ensuring that no escape was possible. I was at last satisfied that the situation was now under control. It had indeed been quite a skirmish.

I suddenly remembered Kim beneath the blanket. She had not moved a muscle since the whole mêlée had begun. I took a tentative step toward her, not really wanting to go there. A picture of her pretty youthful face, a smile ever present, and that long lustrous golden hair, popped into my mind's eye and I was spurred into action. I walked purposely toward the blanket, gently taking it in my mouth to pull it aside. I could feel the eyes of ten dogs, two pups, three duopeds and two horses watching me. The silence was immense, for even the insects seemed to have hushed in anticipation of what I would find.

I took a deep breath and carefully pulled the blanket back from Kim's face. Her eyes were open and for a moment of horror and dread, they looked lifeless. Then, she slowly blinked and a wan smile of recognition fleeted across her small mouth. I barked with joyous abandon and licked her face furiously. A tremendous din arose around me as the dogs began to howl in delight and the pups cheered. Gold Chimes stamped his foreleg upon the ground, waving his head up and down, while DJ neighed with pleasure. We had won, we had finally achieved our goal, and we were not going to let her go this time.

Timothy released his grip on Fur-face, leaving him to Richard's firm hold. He moved across toward the one and only gun visible, and picked it up.

"Ok, guys, you've had it this time! Come, Rich, you'll be better with this than me," he said.

Richard in turn released Fur-face, who sat motionless, eyeing the horses, apparently too terrified to move. He took the weapon from Timothy and trained it upon Goliath.

"One move, and I'll shoot. I've never used one of these before, so I don't know where it'll hit, but I'm not that stupid that it won't hit at all," he said.

"I'm going to fetch some food and water for Kim. Will you be all right on your own?" asked Timothy.

"Are you kidding?" asked Richard, "With Digby's army and two wonderful horses, these guys would be too scared to do anything!"

The dogs barked their enjoyment of that comment and Timothy disappeared into the bushes after removing his McGuyver set and extracting a tiny torch to light his way.

* * * * * * * * * * * * * * * * * * *

When Timothy returned armed with food and water for Kim, the scene had barely changed. I had moved in to keep an eye on Fur-face, but the rest of the animals remained in their places. The two pups assisted Kim to a sitting position and gave her some water from the cup attached to the canister and she sipped delicately. The only item of food that remained was a boiled egg. It was only much later that Kim admitted she ate it grudgingly, being her worst food other than vegetables. She ate it merely to alleviate the terrible hunger that she felt at that moment and had no desire to try another one.

"What now?" Timothy asked.

"We'll have to get Kim back to the farm and somehow get the police here to take care of this lot," said Richard.

It must have been in the middle of the night at this point, so the sound of a police siren out in the wilderness was the last thing any one of us expected.

I have never had a romance in my life, but they say it is never too late. I suppose we are all entitled to have dreams.

Epilogue

I later learned that the police had been following the trail from the cell phone signal. They had lost that at the 'quarry', but used a tracker dog to find their way to the shack. After that it was plain sailing for they soon came across the trashed BMW and not too far along the road, the big four-wheel drive. The tracker dog immediately led them to Irene and Owen who were frantic with worry about the pups, whom they had expected back long before. Once they found the old Ford, they knew they were hot on the trail again. Then they saw the glow from the campfire and the rest is academic.

When I met the tracker dog, I fell in love immediately. Her name is Tina, a stunning looking German Shepherd with sheer guts and determination: a dog of my own heart. I think she rather fancied me too, so with a bit of luck, we might meet up again. I have never had a romance in my life, but they say it is never too late. I suppose we are all entitled to have dreams.

I was delighted to be returned to my home where Ruffles and I were met with such enthusiasm it brought tears to my eyes. Toby and Charlie apparently missed us terribly and wanted to hear the entire tale. Regrettably, Charlie was having great difficulty hearing anything and so I decided to write it all down for her to read, hence "Digby's Diary".

Zimbabwe is located in the southern third of the continent of Africa. The author, Elaine Bird, as well as the artist Miora Briel are from Bulawayo, Zimbabwe. To preserve the flavor of the story, we have left some of the wording and spellings that are different than those of the USA. Do a little research and find out about Zimbabwe and the unique language differences, how many can you find?